# THE RANCHERO'S GIFT

## LAND OF PROMISE SERIES

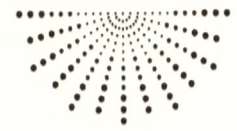

## NANCY J. FARRIER

· River Ink ·

PRESS

*For my husband, Robert John*

*Thank you for your support.*

*For my readers:*

*You are the best*

*Thank you*

# CHAPTER ONE

LOS ANGELES - 1830's

"Papa." Maya Garza yanked against her stepfather's hold to no avail. He dragged her down the street, drawing the stares of men and horses, unaware of the dog trailing in the shadows. Her toe caught on a rut in the road. Bits of dirt flew upward, and she had to hop on one foot for a few steps to catch her balance.

Papa hadn't even given her time to slip on her shoes or fix her braid. Where were they going in such a hurry?

She remembered Ramona, the girl who lived down the street from them. Her father rushed her away one morning, and she'd been married to a *ranchero's* son and moved up north. Something fluttered inside Maya. Would she be married by the end of the day? To someone she didn't know? Hadn't met?

Papa glanced back at her, his face a mask of resolve. She saw nothing in this hard face of the man who'd raised her since she'd been a scared seven-year-old whose father had died. Nothing of the man who encouraged her to read and write, to work figures.

Nothing of the man who told her stories or sang to her when she feared the dark and couldn't sleep.

She saw only the stranger he'd become since misfortune became his companion.

"*Ándele.* Faster." He jerked her arm. "We have to hurry, or I'll miss my chance."

Chance for what? A marriage? Not to any of the sons of her papa's current friends. *Please, no.*

She stumbled into a trot, wanting to ask but afraid to know the answer. Her throat tightened until she could barely breathe, let alone swallow. A leaden ball encased her stomach. The tears she thought she'd seen in her mother's eyes burned in her mind.

Had Mama even tried to change her stepfather's mind? What did she know that Maya didn't?

They rounded a grove of trees and turned onto Olvera Street. She could see the Ávilas' house ahead. She'd gone there before with her father and mother while they'd visited with friends and enjoyed the company of other merchants and landowners.

No longer. Her father didn't have the status now to be in their company. Yet Francisco ÁÁvilaand his *señora*, Encarnación, always treated them with politeness, as if they cared about them. Had her father's loss meant *he* saw others in a different way, not the other way around? Had they requested her presence to work at their home? Her breath caught. Her papa would rush her there if he thought she would bring monetary gain.

"Here."

Papa stopped so suddenly she stumbled into his side. Her breath tumbled in and out, the panting a testimony to her anxiety and their hurried trek.

"Papa, where are we going? Please tell me." Maya hated to plead. Hated to. But she didn't know what else to do. They were destitute, and her stepfather saw this mysterious plan as his only option for getting the money he needed for a new venture. He told Maya she would restore all the wealth they'd had and more. What job could bring enough money to restore what they'd once had?

He always had some scheme to make more money. Each one failed.

Bruno turned to her. "Straighten yourself. Smile." He motioned to her hair, her dress.

She ran her free hand over her hair and down her braid, unable to fix the wayward strands. Her dress wouldn't look better no matter what she did. The ragged lace, the frayed embroidery, the tiny tears. She'd mended and mended, but some things were beyond repair.

A shaggy mutt curled beside the door rose and bared its teeth in a silent snarl, stalking toward them on stiff legs. Maya motioned, and the dog relaxed. She wouldn't have this stray die like so many others. Papa hated her gift with animals and the dogs that always followed her.

Her father kicked dirt at the mutt, and it darted out of reach. He mumbled an expletive and tightened his hold on her upper arm, sending an ache through the limb.

They entered a dim hallway. Emotions fought within her. It was good to get out of the sun's heat. But her stomach clenched at the uncertainty of what lay ahead.

*Oh, Lord, please help me.* If her father meant to marry her off, she'd come without clothing or any of her things. Surely he would have let her pack a bag.

And in this place? She'd heard rumors.

The shadowed room held tables and chairs. Groupings of men sat around the circumference, their low rumble of voices like distant thunder. Maya's knees shook. She picked at a loose thread on her skirt. The bright red of the design had faded since the day she'd finished the work. How long had it been? Her mind fumbled for the useless detail.

"*Señores.*" Her father's voice held little of the usual slur. He hid his drunkenness well. "*Amigos.* I have a treat for you today." He yanked her arm again.

Maya stumbled forward into the shadowed light.

Silence settled over the crowd. The weight of their gazes nearly drove her to her knees. She straightened her spine and her shoulders.

She would not be weak.

Glasses clinked. The smell of tequila hung heavy in the air, even at this hour of the afternoon. Who were the men in this room?

She glanced up and wished she hadn't. As her vision adjusted to the dimness, she could see the men's dark gazes studying her.

Leering at her.

Wanting her.

"Señores, I am in need of funds. Today, I have brought my daughter, Maya. She is a good worker. She is very smart and will learn what you want her to do very fast." Papa paused as a whoop of laughter chased around the room.

What? Maya stared at her father. He wanted to find her work in this cantina? She yanked against his iron grip.

"As you can see, she is very beautiful." With his free hand, her father grasped her chin and turned her head from side to side. Maya tried to jerk free.

Chairs scraped. Clothing rustled. Men crowded closer.

Maya took a half step toward the door, but her stepfather's bruising grip brought her back. This couldn't be what Ramona's father had done with her. Weren't fathers supposed to meet with potential bridegrooms and talk? Why was she here?

"I will sell her to the highest bidder." Papa raised her arm in the air.

*Sell* her? Maya shrank away from him, and swallowed hard. What did Papa mean, sell her? Her gaze darted from the faces to the blocked doorway. *Help me. Please.*

A stranger at her side leaned close. His drooping mustache quivered as he grinned and reached for her.

"No touching the merchandise." Her father wagged his finger at the man. "She can run your household or marry your son. Maya can cook and sew. She is very talented and can entertain your guests."

Laughter rang again. Maya clenched her teeth and fought to breathe. How could he do this? She'd never dreamed he could stoop this low. To sell her like an animal. A slave. Had her mother known? Would no one help her? *God, where are You?*

"Hey, Bruno." A man from the back called over the murmur of the group. "Put her up on a table so we can see what we're getting."

Two of the men hefted a table and carried it to the center of the room. Others made way for them.

"Bring lanterns," another voice called.

The room brightened.

Maya edged toward the shadows. She hunched her shoulders and ducked her head.

Her father—no, her mother's husband—dragged her toward the table. Men circled around, their faces glistening. She'd heard whispers about men who preyed on the helpless. Still, she hadn't believed they could be so depraved. How could they participate in her humiliation? Be so eager to participate?

Hands lifted her to the flat surface, placing her above the crowd. She stumbled. Got her footing. Shifted away from the too-eager fingers. Closed her eyes.

*God, where are You? I need help. Your help.*

He was her only hope. No one else cared what happened to her.

Spurs jingled. Footsteps clumped on the walkway outside the door. Her heart thudded in her chest, and she raised her head. Maybe Señor Ávila had returned early. He would put a stop to this travesty.

Two figures stood in the open doorway. Not Señor Ávila. Not even close. Two young men. Ernesto Cruz, her brother by marriage, and his *compadre*, Rafael Madrigal. Her knees wobbled, and she almost tumbled from the table.

Rafael. Her worst nightmare. In the flesh.

No help would come from them. Rafael probably suggested this plan to her father. He could finally have her in his control. His *esclava*.

His slave.

THE AFTERNOON SUN beat down on Yaniv Madrigal as he rode

toward Olvera Street. He'd planned to be on the road home by now, his chattering hoard of nieces and nephews in tow. Well, only three and a baby, but they felt like a chattering hoard. Trying to keep track of them, to keep them safe, was akin to herding cats. How did their mother deal with the constant worry that something would happen to the little *monstruos?* Adorable monsters, though.

He glanced around. Where was his brother? A not-so-adorable monstruo. Since Rafael hadm't shown up at the specified time, Yaniv had been searching all afternoon. He should have known. He hadn't wanted to bring his wayward brother to town where he could connect with his partner-in-crime, Ernesto. That pair could search out more trouble than a gang of *bandoleros.*

Rafael would have stayed home if their sister hadn't insisted the brothers needed time to get to know one another better now that they were both men. She said their mother would want Yaniv to see they were both important to the family. He snorted. Who took care of the rancho? Who watched over the *familia?* Who went to church and prayed for their souls?

Not Rafael.

Yaniv tied his horse at the hitching post in front of the Ávila house. A roar of raucous male laughter reverberated from the cantina down the street. He frowned. Usually, the hilarity from drinking didn't start this early.

The scent of jasmine wafted toward him as he ascended the steps. His boots clumped on the wooden porch, his spurs jangling a tinny rhythm.

An older woman answered his knock. Her gray hair was pulled back into a tight braid and wound around her head, and she held a broom in one hand. The housekeeper, most likely, who lived with the Ávilas. He didn't know her name.

"I am looking for Señor Ávila. Would you please tell him Yaniv Madrigal is here to see him?" Yaniv swept off his hat and gave a slight bow as he spoke.

"The señor and señora are out of town visiting friends." Her expression darkened as she glanced toward the cantina.

The rough laughter edged across his nerves.

"Thank you." Yaniv placed his hat back on and stepped back into the sunlight. He had hoped Señor Ávila would have word of Rafael and his whereabout—

More laughter. Cheers.

What were those men *doing?*

A heavy sense of dread wormed into the pit of his stomach. Unsavory activity escalated the chance of Rafael and Ernesto being there. He swung onto his horse and headed down the street.

As he entered the cantina, the dimness of the room blinded him, so he stepped to the side of the door until his vision adjusted. No one paid him any attention. All eyes were focused toward the center of the room and some sort of entertainment. Must be good to have every man riveted. Another cheer. Arms raised. Fists pounded tables.

A girl. A young woman. She stood barefoot on the table, not dancing or enticing like the women who usually frequented these places. Her eyes were downcast, her dress worn but not gaudy. She hadn't climbed on that table to have fun. Or to entertain.

"Okay, señores." Bruno Cruz raised his hand from beside the table where the young woman stood. Near him, Yaniv spotted Rafael and his cohort.

"Amigos." Bruno raised his voice. The cacophony died down. "I know you are eager to purchase this señorita, so let's get started.

Who will bid first?" Bruno ignored the chorus of shouts and pointed at his son, Ernesto. "See, my boy is eager to win her. He has opened the bidding."

Bile rose in Yaniv's throat. They were selling this woman? Like a slave? Why?

The blacksmith from the stable pushed through the crowd, heading for the door. The frown on his face and anger in his eyes told much. He caught Yaniv's gaze and motioned outside with a nod of his head.

"What are they doing?" Urgency made Yaniv's tone sharper than he intended. The blacksmith didn't seem to notice.

"Bruno has reached a new low. He is selling his wife's daughter to raise money. Selling her like a piece of livestock." The blacksmith spat in the dust. "I'll have none of it. You would do well to drag your brother out of there and get away from here." He stalked down the street without a backward glance.

"What about the woman?"

More laughter and cheers surged through the open door. Two more men exited, disgust on their faces. Most stayed.

Yaniv stepped back inside. He should grab Rafael and leave. He should. His brother stood close to the woman, his gaze riveted on her. He had no money. Certainly not enough to purchase a woman. Or did he?

Yaniv wove through the crowd. He would be on his way soon with his brother in tow—

Through loose strands of the woman's hair, he caught the glint of tears.

Her eyes found him. Fear pinched her lips. Pleading shimmered in her eyes. Desperation. Rafael had his fist around her bare ankle.

His fingers were dark against her paler skin. Yaniv watched as she tried to break free. And failed.

"Rafael." Yaniv grasped his brother's shoulder and pulled him around. "We must go."

His *hermano's* eyes were glazed and took a moment to focus. He released the woman's ankle. "Yaniv. I can't go." He grabbed Yaniv by the shirtfront as he reached back to brush his fingers up the woman's lower leg. "You have to give me more money. I must have her."

"Have her? Are you *loco?*" And their sister thought this boy grown up. He wanted to shake some values and morals into him. As if that were an option.

"If I don't buy her, someone else will. I can't lose her." Rafael glanced back, pounding his fist against his leg when Bruno shouted for more bids. The room had quieted. The bidding must have gone too high for most of these fools.

"This is not your business." Yaniv tugged at Rafael. "We must go. Now." The weight of the woman's despair beat at him. He couldn't risk a look at her. Had to get his brother away. Get himself away.

"Go, Rafe." Ernesto's encouragement sounded more like a jeer. "I will keep her and tell you about the fun I have when this one is mine."

Rafael raised his hand for another bid.

A strangled sound escaped the woman. Yaniv wouldn't have heard but for the sudden silence in the room. He glanced up, his hold still tight on his brother.

Luminous brown eyes stared down at him. In this low light, her gaze was nearly black. Despite how some of her braid had loosened and fallen around her face, he could still see her. A gaunt face emphasized her high cheekbones. Had she been without food, or did terror give her such an appearance?

He took in her heart-shaped face. Her bowed lips. The strength in the set of her shoulders.

She smiled. Not a full smile. A small tipping of the mouth. A sign of hope in the midst of hopelessness.

"Is that the final bid?" Bruno's shout brought him back to the events at hand. "She will go to Rafael if no one raises the bid."

No. He couldn't help her. Not with his responsibilities. To his family. The ranch. To God—

Yaniv raised his hand.

# CHAPTER TWO

"Stay out of this!" Rafael surged toward Yaniv, his face darkened, and his eyes narrowed. Hands fisted, he stopped in front of Yaniv, jaw jutting.

Ernesto grasped his friend's shoulder and pulled him back a step.

"Maya is *mine*." Rafael ground out the words. "I have saved for this."

"You want to buy your best friend's sister? Why not ask for her hand in marriage? Why humiliate her?" Yaniv forced his own hands to unclench. He would not get in a fight. Not with his own brother. Not in front of this crowd.

"She needed to learn a lesson." Ernesto stepped forward beside his friend. He jerked his head, his messy hair flipping back from his forehead. He had an inch-long scar above his right eyebrow. From fighting? Did he enjoy the sport? Some men did.

"What kind of a *lesson* calls for belittling a person?"

At Yaniv's question, a murmur ran through the crowd of men. Disgust clawed at his throat. Minutes ago they were all willing participants in the show. Now they acted like they had nothing to do with mistreating Maya.

"Gentlemen." Bruno hopped off the chair to clap his son on the back. "Let's start the bidding again. We must finish this before tonight's meal. Right?" His forced laugh fell flat in the now-silent room.

"This *ranchero* needs to leave first." Ernesto motioned toward Yaniv with his chin. "He has no part in this."

Bruno leaned close to whisper in his son's ear, but the words carried: "His money is as good as another's."

The young woman edged to the side of the table. Yaniv noted the men on the far side had moved so an open space yawned between the table and the door. Was she fast enough to get away before her brother or Rafael caught her?

She took another step. He kept his gaze from drifting her direction. He didn't want anyone else to notice her plan to escape.

The cantina had warmed to the point of stifling. Men's sweat and the sharp tang of alcohol hung in the air. The girl shuffled sideways again. Her dirt-encrusted toes pressed into the table top. Yaniv held his breath. He tried to think of something to say. A distraction. A way to give her a moment's head start.

Bruno glanced her direction. "Hey!"

Rafael whirled as Maya leaped. He struck like a snake, grabbing her ankle before she completed her jump. She fell. Her leg jerked from his grasp. They all heard the thump and whoosh of air as she hit the floor.

Yaniv pushed Ernesto back into his father. He shoved his brother the other way and rounded the now-empty table.

*Please don't let her be hurt, God.*

He burned at the thought of one of his sisters—of any woman—being treated in such a despicable manner.

He knelt beside her. She blinked up at him as blood leaked from a cut on her lip. A large tear in her skirt gave a glimpse of her shapely leg. Yaniv looked away, embarrassed for her.

"Are you hurt? Can you sit up?" He held out his hand to her.

"Get up." Rafael had rounded the table on the other side of her. Ernesto stood beside him.

"Get up." Rafael aimed a kick at her side, and Yaniv grabbed his brother's foot and twisted. Rafael's arms wind-milled as he tried to stay upright. Ernesto caught him from behind, steadying him. Yaniv released his boot.

"If you try to kick her again, I will take you outside and teach you the manners you should have learned long ago." He glared at Rafael. What had happened that he missed their padre's lessons on how to treat a woman. How to treat a *human?*

Another round of murmurs ran through the cantina. Likely those who saw the interaction were relaying to others what had happened. These fools may have been willing to go along with the bidding on a girl, but he doubted they'd go along with hurting her.

"What is your top bid?" Bruno's voice rang out in the quiet. He flinched, then stepped away to confer with Ernesto and Rafael.

The young woman pushed up to a sitting position. "Thank you, señor." Her face reddened as she noted the tear in her skirt. She pulled the pieces together, twisting them in her trembling fingers.

"Let me help you out of here." Yaniv rose to his feet and again offered his hand. "You need to go back home."

Before they reached the door, Rafael and Ernesto blocked their way. His brother's eyes burned, though whether at the woman or him, Yaniv couldn't tell.

"Let go of Maya." Ernesto reached for her. "You have not won the bidding. You have no right to her."

"She needs to go home to her mother. You shouldn't be trying to sell her. I will ask the Ávilas' housekeeper to see her home."

Maya's wrist resembled a fragile bird's wing in his grasp. He didn't want to release her, but he couldn't get into a tug-of-war over her.

"Her mother doesn't want her anymore. She is nothing but trouble." Bruno shoved him aside, picked Maya up, and set her back up on the table. He raised his voice. "We will start the bidding again where we left off." He named the amount of Rafael's last bid, ignoring Yaniv's and any following offers to buy Maya.

"Yaniv's bid was higher." One man in the back of the crowd lifted his voice.

"You will leave." Rafael stepped up to Yaniv.

"This is none of your business." Ernesto flanked his friend.

"I thought this auction was a public one, not private." He met Rafael's burning gaze. "Is that right, Bruno? She is your wife's daughter. You set the rules."

"He said anyone could bid." The voice from the back sounded like the earlier one. "Everyone's money is good."

Bruno stretched up to stare through the crowd, a frown darkening his face. He turned to Yaniv. "You may bid." He ignored the glare his son shot at him as he climbed onto a chair. "Does anyone offer more than Rafael? She is healthy. A good seamstress. She can read and do figures. She will make a good wife." Bruno pursed his lips and wagged his head back and forth. "Or perhaps you have another use for her."

Yaniv thought of the money he'd saved to buy a special horse on this trip. A horse he didn't need.

"My bid is the most. She is *mine.*" Rafael reached for Maya. His face glowed with an unholy light.

Maya's eyes shone with a mix of fear and defiance. Mostly fear.

"I'll raise my bid." Yaniv's pronouncement cut the chatter as he named his price. A shockwave ran through the room.

The chair wobbled as Bruno shifted and almost fell. He caught his balance. Greed gleamed in his eyes as his gaze swung around the room.

Rafael had grabbed Ernesto and was saying something urgent to him. Ernesto shook his head and held out his hands, palms open. If Rafael wanted money from his friend, he wouldn't get it. The amigos were one and the same. Money ran from their grasp like water through a sieve.

His brother shook off Ernesto's hand and stalked toward Yaniv. Men around them were talking again, some betting on who would purchase the woman. Yaniv's anger simmered.

Rafael bent close to him. "Walk. Away."

The sour stench of tequila washed over Yaniv. He refused to back off.

Spittle sprayed from his brother's lips. "Leave her to me! Withdraw your offer. Why do you need this girl?"

He met his brother's eyes. "I will not let you have her. You have no business buying a woman." Yaniv pushed his brother back a step.

"And you do?" Rafael grabbed his brother's arm.

MAYA'S BREATH caught in her throat. Maybe they would fight. If so, she could slip away in the chaos. Rafael's brother spoke truth. She could find safety with Rosalie, the Ávilas' housekeeper. No one would think of crossing that threshold for something this base.

She'd only seen Yaniv Madrigal the few times he'd come to their *hacienda* on business. He hadn't seen her, but she'd watched him. His quiet authority and handsome face had drawn her. She could tell he didn't like her father.

No. Not her father. Not anymore.

*Bruno.*

She inched toward the edge of the table as men circled the brothers. She had an opening leading to the door. Her fingers twisted in her skirt. Her muscles tensed. A hand grabbed her ankle.

Bruno glared up at her. "You won't escape. This day you will be sold and no more be my concern." His voice pitched low, he leaned toward her so his words wouldn't carry. "Your mother will not be sorry to see you go."

His barb struck deep. Her heart thudded. Truth? Did he speak truth? She and her mother had often been at odds, but her mother loved her. Didn't she?

A roar from the men jerked her from her reverie. Rafael threw a punch at his brother. Yaniv caught the fist and twisted it. Pain shot across Rafael's face.

Maya tried to tamp down the joy she shouldn't be feeling. How many times had she wanted Ernesto's friend to get his comeuppance? Too many to count.

Yaniv released his brother with a dire warning. "Leave here. Go to the camp. We are ready to travel." He shoved Rafael toward the door. "I will meet you there."

Ernesto clapped Rafael's shoulder, and the pair headed out into the afternoon sunshine. Brightness slivered through the doorway as they left. Oh, to flee through that door! To run to freedom and safety. The door swung closed, restoring the dimness of the cantina.

"Will anyone else top Yaniv's bid?" Bruno attempted to enact his former bravado, but she could hear the quaver in his voice. Others seemed to as well.

Men turned away. Where once they had been groping for her, now they acted disinterested.

Relief surged—

Then crashed as she realized she had been sold to a man.

Yaniv stepped close to Bruno, and money changed hands. Bruno's calculating gaze tracked from Yaniv to Maya. She didn't have to think hard to know he wanted to wring more money from this man. How many times or ways did he intend to sell her?

"Take note, Cruz." Yaniv stepped close to Bruno. "You will not do this again. You will not mistreat another woman. If you do, I will hear about it and come for you. Do you understand?"

Fear widened Bruno's eyes. He stepped back. "I needed money. That is all."

"You need to work and not gamble." Disgust drew Yaniv's brows together as he stared at her former father. "If you put in half the time working that you do drinking with your compadres, you would still have a thriving business."

Maya glanced around. Many of her father's...*Bruno's* compadres were here. They were across the room now, talking and drinking, paying no attention as he received his comeuppance. *Thank heaven.* Yaniv's censure could bring Bruno trouble if he didn't do as he was told.

"My business is none of yours." Bruno's chin jutted out as she'd seen it do many times. The same defiance had been in Ernesto when she'd told him to leave her alone. Which was not nearly as frightening as the lack of emotion she noted in Rafael when she pushed him away. What would she do when Yaniv took her with him and she had to be around his brother every day?

Would she ever be free?

From slavery?

From fear?

Not once could she remember being free to choose what she wanted to do. First, her mother controlled her. Then Bruno. Then Ernesto. She shuddered. Ernesto and Rafael were the worst. The pair sought to trap her alone anytime they were together.

If Yaniv hadn't interceded on her behalf... Bitterness filled her mouth. At least in Yaniv, she saw some semblance of compassion. Perhaps his ownership wouldn't be as bad as it could have been with so many others.

"Get down." Bruno yanked on her skirt. The fabric pulled from her grasp and the tear gaped open to reveal her leg. Heat burned her face as she twisted the material together. Bruno jerked her to the floor, and she stumbled. A hand steadied her.

Yaniv.

The warmth of his touch skittered through her. She ducked her head, too embarrassed to meet his gaze. What must he think of her? Cast off like trash. She couldn't bear the thought.

"Take her from here." Bruno's low growl made her shudder.

Her only hope was to get away from Los Angeles. Going with Yaniv meant going with Rafael.

*Tapar un hoyo y destapar otro.*

To fill one hole while digging another.

Bruno's compadres turned to watch as she followed Yaniv out the door. The weight of their gazes pushed against her, and she fought to quell a surge of nausea.

She squinted against the brightness of the sun. Her eyes watered, and she blinked the moisture away, not wanting Yaniv to see it as weakness. A light breeze caressed her cheek and lifted stray strands of hair from her neck. She must look a mess. If only the ground would open up and swallow her.

"Do you have somewhere to go?" Yaniv's question caught her by surprise.

"To go?" She swiped strands of hair from her face and stared up at him.

His dark eyes shone with compassion. His handsome cheeks were shadowed with stubble. His broad shoulders offered protection for the right person.

"I am to go with you. Aren't I?" Her heart thudded a heavy beat. Had she missed something? Had this man given her back to her father?

Would she be sold again tomorrow?

A nightmare revisited?

"Here." He pressed a paper into her hand. "This paper shows you are free. Free to do what you want."

Chills snaked down her spine at the low chuckle behind her.

# CHAPTER THREE

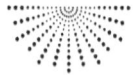

"Free?" Maya's voice squeaked on a high note. She glanced to the side trying to find the source of the sound she'd heard. Nothing moved.

"Yes." Yaniv stepped toward a pinto mare tied to a post. "I give you your freedom, Maya. You can do whatever you want. Go wherever you want."

She stared at him. No one had ever said she could do what she wanted to. Her mother, her stepfather, even her young brothers all ordered her around as if her sole reason for existence was to serve them.

She fisted her skirt as chills washed over her. Bumps pebbled down her arms. Where was she to go? She had nowhere. Nowhere safe. If she returned home, Bruno would sell her again. He wouldn't care about a worthless piece of paper. Not when he could get more money and be rid of a mouth to feed.

"Wait." Maya leaped forward as he swung onto the mare. "Please."

The pinto swung her head around to blow a warm breath across

Maya's arm. She stroked the horse's muzzle as she stared up into Yaniv's handsome face. She fumbled for words. What would make him understand?

Maybe she should let him go. Maybe Señora Ávila would give her a job. She'd promise to work hard. She always worked hard.

Movement at the corner of the building caught her attention again. Rafael came out of the shadows to lean one shoulder against the adobe. His face twisted with a leering grin. He must know his brother didn't want her. He would snatch her up as soon as Yaniv left. She didn't stand a chance of escaping him.

"Please." She turned to stare back up at Yaniv.

His gaze had strayed to the corner where his brother loitered. His brow furrowed. Dark stubble gave him a rakish appearance, yet she'd seen the kindness of his heart. She liked the way he looked.

"Take me with you. I will work hard. I can do many things. Cook. Clean. Sew." She paused, fighting tears. He *had* to understand.

"You offered me freedom. I choose to go with you." She clutched his stirrup. The horse stomped a hoof perilously close to her foot. The dirt puffed up and drifted over her toes. The dog across the street trotted toward her. Ernesto stepped up beside Rafael and pitched a rock at the mutt. The dog yelped and ran.

Maya tried not to cry. She kept her gaze riveted on Yaniv. His mouth thinned, and he jerked his gaze from his brother back to her. She held her breath, afraid even to pray for help.

"We are traveling today. First to a friend's rancho and then back home. Are you able to help with the cooking and the children?"

"Yes." Her knees wobbled. She tightened her hold on the stirrup. If she let go, she would collapse to the ground.

His intense focus pierced her soul. She wanted to look away but didn't dare. What would he see? The same worthlessness Bruno saw?

The innocence the men in the cantina bid on?

The girl who longed for acceptance and love?

Or who she really was--a woman who needed to escape her life of fear and slavery?

He held out his hand. Strong fingers clasped hers, and he swung her up behind him. "My sister will be glad to have the company. And the help with her *niños.*"

She tried not to sag against him. She glanced down and froze. The ground seemed so far away. Her body shook so badly she feared she would spook his mount. She didn't want to tell him she'd never been on a horse before. She averted her gaze from the corner of the building where Rafael's anger radiated like lightning. She would focus on Yaniv's back and not on Rafael or the long drop.

Yaniv clicked his tongue, and his pinto ambled forward and then stopped. Maya clutched the loose folds of his shirt and tried to balance.

"Rafael, I'll expect you at the wagons within the hour. Don't make me come look for you again." Yaniv's directive brooked no argument.

Maya peeked from under lashes to see Rafael sneer at his brother. Only a slight jerk of his head acknowledged the order.

Another click of the tongue. The mare shifted into a bumpy trot as they exited Olvera Street and headed to the edge of town. Almost bouncing off, Maya gripped Yaniv tighter. The gait smoothed into a canter. She caught the rhythm and relaxed.

She didn't look back. With every hoofbeat, her fear drifted farther away. She'd never been so light and free. Ever.

The fleeting thought of her mother saddened her. Yet her mother had let Maya be sold to the highest bidder. She hadn't even begged Bruno for her daughter's freedom. She'd remained emotionless as he dragged Maya from the house.

How could it be that freedom had come through a stranger? One who didn't know her but showed compassion anyway. She didn't know Yaniv. Had never spoken to him. Yet she would give her life to him for the gift he'd given her.

"Where is your home?" She lifted her face to the clean breeze as she spoke.

Yaniv slowed the mare to a walk.

"Our rancho is a few days' travel southeast of here." He gestured vaguely with his hand. The pinto snorted and jangled her bridle. "Sometimes I wish we were farther from Los Angeles."

She understood. If he lived farther from town, maybe his brother wouldn't be so tempted to consort with Ernesto.

Yaniv went on. "We are going to the Armenta Rancho before we go home. That will make the trip longer, but I need to do some business with the Don and his son, Lucio. Do you know the Armenta familia?" His resonating baritone calmed her frayed nerves. Exhaustion from the tension of the day weighing her down, she relaxed even further.

"I met Don Armenta one time when my *madre* and pa...Bruno took me to the Ávilas'. He had a very beautiful horse. He may even have been to our house when I was younger. I didn't always know the men my stepfather did business with."

"The Armentas are known for their horses, whose beauty and

stamina are unmatched in Alta California. I am buying some new stock for our rancho. Lucio sent a message to me that they have several mares for sale."

Her forehead bumped against his back. His shirt, roughened and slightly damp, smelled of him. Not a bad smell. Not the stench of so many men who visited her stepfather to do business with him. Or the alcoholic stink of the men in the cantina. She fought a shiver. How often had Bruno paraded her through the room on the pretense of having her serve his friends their meal or drinks?

No more. She'd been freed from that horror.

She hoped.

Her eyelids drifted down. She needed to sit up and be alert. Her body wouldn't obey.

She knew nothing until the pinto halted and the noise of people chattering startled her awake.

"You *bought* a woman, Yaniv!" The indignation in the woman's voice made Maya cringe and keep her eyes closed. Her muscles tightened in response to the change she felt in Yaniv's posture.

"Shh, Helida." Yaniv's low tone vibrated through his back to Maya's forehead.

"Don't you quiet me." Helida's voice shrilled.

Maya's face burned as she pictured the whole camp staring at them.

"Rafael told me what you did."

Yaniv jerked, and Maya gasped. Rafael had gotten to the camp before them to spread his hatred. She shuddered and cracked her eyes open to glance around, trying to keep from looking at Helida.

She could only imagine the anger and disgust on the woman's face.

"You! You always talk to the children, to all of us, about doing what is right." Helida's voice lowered to a near whisper. "What is right about buying a slave girl?"

YANIV STARED down at his incensed and mistaken sister. He wasn't surprised Rafael had beaten them back to the camp. He'd gone slower than usual with Maya's weight against his back and the symphony of her deep breathing lulling him.

He had enjoyed those moments far more than he would admit to anyone. If asked, he would say he hadn't wanted to jar her. She'd suffered a difficult day, more than even he could imagine. Where had her mother been? Why hadn't she objected to her daughter being sold off for who-knew-what purpose? Some of those men....

"Helida." He had to bite his lip to keep from chuckling at the outrage of her expression. Right now he would fear going to sleep. She might well murder him in his bed.

Her chin jutted out even more as she tried to stare him down. Her flashing eyes and hands on hips reminded him so much of his mother when he and his brothers provoked her ire.

"Just what do you mean bringing her here? What are your plans?" Helida's long braid slid over her shoulder when she jerked her head.

"If you give me some time, I will explain." Yaniv turned to take Maya's arm and help her from the horse. He swung down to stand beside her. The top of her head didn't even come to his shoulder.

She gripped the torn parts of her skirt, twining them together. He drew in a deep breath and shook off wayward thoughts.

A horse neighed in the distance, and his mare's sides puffed out as she whinnied back. Distant laughter and the sounds of the *vaqueros* called to him. He had work to do and needed his sister to trust him. When had he ever let anyone down or done anything against the law?

"I'm listening." Helida's body all but vibrated from her anger.

Maya inched closer, hiding behind him. He couldn't blame her. His sister could be terrifying to those who didn't know her.

And to those who did.

"First, think about who told you I purchased Maya." Yaniv noted Helida's gaze shot to the side and knew his brother was behind him somewhere. "Then consider my character and what I stand for."

Her lips pursed. Her shoulders relaxed a fraction. Maya's fingers twisted the side of his shirt.

"So you're saying you didn't buy this girl?" Helida tilted her head to the side.

"I bought her." When she stiffened again, Yaniv held up his hand. "But she is not my slave." Off to the side, he heard Rafael snort.

His sister frowned, then turned her lethal gaze to Maya. "Is he telling the truth? Did he buy you?"

As if she'd had a sudden infusion of courage, Maya stepped away from him and closer to Helida. She swept her wayward hair back with her free hand. "He saved me."

Her chin lifted, almost matching his sister's stance. "If Yaniv hadn't purchased me, I would have been at the mercy of that scoundrel, Rafael. Your brother set me free."

He couldn't resist a glance at said scoundrel. Rafael's face resembled a thundercloud. Yaniv lifted his brows and cocked his head. Rafael almost growled. He understood Yaniv's implied slight.

"How old are you?" Helida asked Maya. "You look like you should still be home with your madre. Where are your parents?"

"They sold me." Maya's quiet statement sent a hush throughout the camp. Even the horses were silent. The stench of dead fires and manure hung in the air.

Yaniv ached for the señorita. He'd hoped her mother hadn't been around or hadn't felt safe trying to keep Bruno in check. His fist tightened, pushing the reins into his palm.

He reached out to touch her but stopped. She'd been mistreated and didn't need some man trying to take control of her again. He'd promised her freedom, and he would see she had her choice of where to go and what she wanted to do. If he had the power to do so.

Helida relaxed. It was clear she saw Maya's hurt. He'd been right to bring Maya here. His sister would take her under her very capable wing and show her the love she showed everyone. Well…

Everyone who behaved themselves.

He glanced at Rafael. And a few who didn't.

The two women walked off. He heard Helida talking about helping Maya repair her dress and finding shoes for her to wear. Yaniv led his mare toward the wagons to see if the vaqueros were ready to pull out. Rafael fell into step beside him. He loved his brother. He did. But he often didn't like him very much.

"You think you have won, hermano." Rafael's snarl carried a

warning he didn't miss. "You haven't. She will be mine. I have waited a long time for this one, and you will not have her."

Waited a long time? Yaniv kept his expression from showing his disgust. Maya might be a woman, but she wasn't much past girlhood. How long had Rafael been after her?

"Stay away from her." He faced his brother. His pinto brushed her nose across his shoulder, and her warm breath fanned his neck. "You are not to bother her at all. Is that understood?"

Rafael grinned—the grin that always made Madre and his sisters give in to him. "You can't deny *amor*, mi hermano. True love will win."

Yaniv snorted. "You wouldn't know true love if it hit you between the eyes." He shook his head. "Go bring me the little sorrel mare we let the kids ride. I don't think Maya has ridden much, so I want her to have a gentle mount. We don't have room for her on the wagons."

Rafael puffed out his chest. "She can ride with me."

"She can ride on her own. Now go. Bring the mare." Yaniv strode off toward the vaqueros, who waited by the wagons. If he stayed by his brother any longer, he might be tempted to tie him to his horse with a gag in his mouth.

"She will want to ride with me by tomorrow," Rafael called after him. The man had to get in the last word. Had to.

Yaniv didn't turn around. He refused to give his brother the satisfaction.

THEY WERE on the road in thirty minutes. They were late and had to cover a few miles to stay at a friend's rancho on the way to the

Armentas. Yaniv sent one of the vaqueros on ahead to give an estimate of when they would arrive.

He should have sent his brother as well. Since they'd left Los Angeles, Rafael had pressed his suit with Maya. He pursued her like most men would hunt a deer. Maya struggled to stay astride the mare and out of Rafael's reach. A vaquero had alerted Yaniv to the drama going on. Helida hadn't noticed. She must be too distracted by her children to see Rafael's escapades.

Yaniv urged his mare to pick up the pace. As he approached, his brother sidled his mount next to Maya's and reached for her. Maya leaned away from him and lost her balance.

She scrabbled for the pommel of the saddle.

Dipped to the side.

Toppled.

A cloud of dirt puffed up when she landed hard. Her mare danced sideways into Rafael's horse. He was almost unseated. Anger darkened his face. He jerked his horse to a stop and leaped from the saddle, stalking toward Maya.

# CHAPTER FOUR

HER BREATH WHOOSHED OUT. Pain radiated through her body. She couldn't breathe. How could it hurt so much to fall from such a small horse? She gasped. Dragged in air. Coughed on the dust floating around her.

She pushed against the ground, biting back a groan as she sat up. She glanced up to see Rafael storming toward her, looking blacker than a moonless night. She scooted backward. Stopped. Gathered her hastily mended skirt and stumbled upright on unsteady legs. He could not intimidate her. Well, he could, but she refused to let him know it.

"Stop right there." Yaniv flung himself from his horse, landing in front of Maya. She hadn't even seen him coming, yet here he was, so close she could almost rest her forehead against his back. Again.

She fought the urge to do so.

"Get out of my way." Rafael's growl scraped her nerves. "This is my business with the slave girl, not yours."

Before she could register the insult, Yaniv had his brother's shirt in his fist, collar twisted in a chokehold, and Rafael's face had darkened. Maya stumbled back and stared at the brothers. They were like day and night. Light and dark...

Good and evil?

Maybe Rafael wasn't evil—yet. But, he had a darkness in him that might lead to ruin if he didn't change.

"Maya does not belong to you. Do you understand, mi hermano?" Yaniv's jaw muscles bunched as he waited for an answer.

Rafael didn't appear able to respond. His hands circled Yaniv's wrists. His eyes bugged out as his face purpled.

"Stop!" Maya leaped forward to put her hand on Yaniv's arm. The shiver of revulsion from being this close to her nemesis vied with the tingle of awareness at touching Yaniv. "Let him go."

They stood in a frozen tableau for a long moment. Yaniv dragged his gaze from his brother to look at her. She could see comprehension returning. His hold relaxed.

Rafael sucked in air. Jerked free. Coughed. Bent over, hands on his knees as he dragged in one breath after another.

Her hand still on Yaniv's sleeve, Maya felt the change in his posture as much as she saw from the corner of her eye. She pulled her hand back. He bent his head and rubbed at his face.

He trained a hard gaze on her. "Are you hurt?" He reached toward her, but she stepped back. He may have been nice enough up to now, and she owed him plenty, but he was Rafael's brother. Could she trust him?

"It's nothing." The twinge in her side belied her statement, but she didn't let the pain show on her face. She'd had worse from Bruno.

He always said Maya's strong will needed a sharp slap to keep her in line. He hadn't been afraid to exact the punishment and more.

The sorrel mare stretched out her neck and nuzzled Maya's arm. She stroked the horse's nose.

Yaniv focused on Rafael, who had regained some of his bravado. "You will stay away from Maya. I don't want you to ride close to her or even talk to her. Do you understand?"

Rafael's lips curled in a sneer. "You think because you paid the price, she is yours." His chin jutted toward Yaniv. "You'll find I don't give up that easily. She will be mine someday because you don't want her. I heard you set her free."

"¡Ya basta! Stop it!" Maya waved her hand at the brothers. She winced at the jolt of pain in her side. She tried not to.

Rafael didn't notice.

Yaniv did.

He reached for her, but she lifted her hand, palm out. He halted.

She ignored Rafael and focused on Yaniv. "If you would help me up on the horse, we need to catch up."

He swiveled to look at the wagons drawing away from them. Sounds of the children asking questions drifted back. Maya knew they were asking questions because that is all they had done all day. Helida had so much patience with her little ones.

"She's right." Yaniv narrowed his eyes at his brother. "Go make sure the livestock and wagons get to the proper camping spot. We're almost there. I'll help Maya mount up."

She could tell Rafael wanted to argue. Indecision warred across his handsome features. Features similar to Yaniv's, yet softer and more rounded. He turned, grabbed his mount's reins, and leaped into the saddle in one smooth motion. His gaze raked across her before he turned and cantered after the rest of the group.

Yaniv stared after him, his jaw muscles bunching and releasing. His sculpted cheeks were covered with stubble. Dark hair fell across his forehead. He reached down to snatch his hat from where it had fallen in the dirt, banged the brim against his leg, and put it back on.

He turned to Maya. "Now, tell me the truth. I know you are hurt, but how bad? Do I need to get Helida or one of the other women to help you?"

"No. It's no worse than—" Heat flooded her face. She'd almost revealed a secret known only to her and her family. "I'm not used to riding a horse. I'm sore is all."

"You are very brave. And you inspire something in animals. First my pinto and now the sorrel. They all seem to love you." His slow smile made her pulse beat faster. He strode toward the small horse, grabbed the reins, and turned her for Maya to mount. "We are almost at our camp for the night. You'll be able to rest. I believe Helida has some ointment that will help with the soreness."

He lifted her as if she weighed nothing and swung her up onto the saddle. She bit her lip as her sore muscles and her side screamed in protest. He held onto the reins. She needed to reach for them and gather the courage to try guiding this mare again. The horse had been sweet and gentle, but Maya wanted to be off of her for the night more than she wanted to eat or sleep.

"Just hold on." Yaniv's hand covered hers where she gripped the pommel of the saddle. "I'll lead your horse, and you only have to stay on. Okay?"

He swung astride his pinto, and they moved off at a slow pace.

Each step jarred her and chafed the sore spots. She would not show her discomfort.

She. Would. Not.

When Yaniv glanced back at her, she did her best to smile, although her expression probably resembled more of a death grimace than anything pleasant.

They rode in a comfortable silence. He didn't fill every moment bragging about his various escapades or suggesting what he intended to do with her.

Night and day.

How could two brothers be so completely different?

The sun at their backs dipped below the horizon as the shadows lengthened to dusk. A cool breeze caressed away the heat of the day. The sweet scent of primrose permeated the air, and she breathed in the fragrance, relaxing for the second time today.

Something about Yaniv touched her. She'd never met a man like him. He paid the price for her and then set her free. He'd been kind. Thoughtful. Protective. Though he didn't know her at all, he seemed to care for her.

Gratitude bloomed within her. Had he been God's answer to her panicked prayer? Moisture burned her eyes, but she would not cry. He would never understand her tears were of joy. Instead, she vowed to do whatever she could to repay him for his gift of kindness.

Somehow she would repay him for all he'd sacrificed.

Yaniv lifted Maya down from the mare and watched her make

her way slowly across camp. Her stiff gait told him how much she hurt. Tomorrow would be worse. By morning her sore muscles would be in full protest. Sitting on a horse all day tomorrow would be even worse for her. Yet with her determination, she would not complain.

He gave instructions to a boy for tending their horses and strode toward his sister. Helida could help him figure a way to keep Maya off her horse tomorrow. How had the señorita not learned to ride? Everyone on his ranch, even his abuela, knew how to ride. They might not go often, but they knew how. Maya acted as if she'd never been on a horse before.

One of the vaqueros motioned him over to see a problem with a wagon. By the time he'd finished figuring out a temporary solution, Yaniv looked over to see Helida helping with supper at the cook fire. He didn't see Maya or Rafael and tried to tamp down his concern. Helida would know where she'd disappeared to.

"Hermano." Helida patted him on the cheek as his mother had for years. His chest tightened as the memory of his mother and the ache of losing her washed over him anew.

"Your señorita is okay." She grinned. "I can see it in your face and the way your eyes roam around the camp searching for her. I think Rafael has some competition."

"Rafael is to stay away from her. He has no business being near Maya." Yaniv clamped his teeth together, regretting the snarl in his voice. Helida didn't seem to mind. She gave him a knowing look before giving an order to one of the girls turning meat on the fire.

"Over there." Helida nodded toward a stand of trees.

Yaniv could see Maya walking back and forth in the lengthening shadows, bouncing the baby in her arms.

"I gave her some salve. Then I gave her the chore of walking the baby because the movement will help more than the ointment. *La bebe* has been teething and is running a fever. Tomorrow, I will have Maya ride in the wagon with her while I corral the rest of the niños."

He wanted to give his sister a hug, but he'd never been one to show much affection. He touched her shoulder and saw she understood. Giving Maya an excuse to ride in the wagon would save her pride and give her extra time to heal. Maybe the following day she could ride for a few hours. To make the journey easier, he would ride alongside and instruct her. By the time they reached the Armenta rancho, she would be well settled into the art of being a horsewoman.

"Thank you, Helida. Do you need anything else?" He turned away even as he asked, drawn toward Maya like a parched man to water.

"One thing." Helida's tone halted him. She waited until he faced her again. "Rafael is not such a bad sort. He's young. Remember, he's your brother."

Her words of caution speared him with guilt and with anger. She hadn't seen the way their brother had acted with Maya. The lust that lit his eyes as he gazed at the young woman. The excitement that lit his face. The utter loathing as Yaniv won the bid. He had no idea how to tell Helida their baby brother had wrong motives. She'd never been able to see anything bad in Rafael.

As he strode toward Maya, the rest of the camp—the odors of manure, sweat, and smoke, and the sounds of animals and people —faded away. Even the fussy niña Maya bounced in her arms didn't bother him. His only thought was to reach Maya. To tell her where she would stay. To inquire about how she felt.

To be close to her once again.

He could still feel the spot in the middle of his back where her head rested as she slept on the way to camp. He had no idea why she inspired such feelings in him. He wanted to protect her from ever being hurt again. He wanted to keep her close. He wanted...

He shook the thoughts from his head.

"Would you like me to take her?" He held out his arms for the fussy Ana. The little one lunged toward him, and Maya almost dropped her. Yaniv scooped the child up into his arms, tugged his handkerchief from his pocket, and wiped her nose. Ana turned her head, her wailing growing louder.

Relief showed in Maya's face as she shook her arms, turning a little as she did so. He bit back a smile. She didn't want him to see how this chunky little girl had tired her. He could only imagine the stress she had endured this day. Still, she kept on, giving of herself and not complaining.

As the baby settled in and nestled against his shoulder, Yaniv walked into the trees. Maya stayed beside him. When he looked at her, he could see the tilt of her nose. The brush of her long lashes against her dusky cheek. The red of her full lips. So beautiful. No wonder Rafael wanted her for his own. He'd always liked fine things.

"I wanted to tell you about our sleeping arrangements when we are traveling." He saw her start and regretted his wording. "The women all sleep together in one area. Helida will help you find bedding and a safe place to rest."

Her shoulders relaxed a fraction. Her lips parted as she released a breath.

"If you have any more trouble with Rafael, please come to me. I'll try to watch, but he is pretty crafty." He paused. Should he say more?

"Rafael came late to my parents. He was born after my mother had several stillborn children. Needless to say, my parents and my sisters pampered him. I don't think that has been good for him." Yaniv patted Ana's back as her breathing deepened and she relaxed against him.

"I just want him to leave me alone." Maya's voice caught. She bit her lip, her hands closed in fists.

In the distance, a bell rang. Yaniv turned back toward camp. Their dinner would be ready. Maya stayed alongside him as if she knew his steps before he took them.

As they approached the camp, he could see the vaqueros seated waiting to be served, the lantern light creating a soft glow. The women were busy taking plates of food to the men. One of them carried a large pot of coffee to fill mugs.

Rafael sat alone. He glared at Yaniv for a moment, then stared at Maya. When a woman handed him a plate, he took it without looking at her. The weight of his gaze didn't waver from the girl walking beside Yaniv.

Maya's whole attitude changed. She stiffened. Her shoulders straightened. Her bearing became that of a lady demanding respect. Yaniv almost laughed at the look on his brother's face. Rafael had met his match. Maya wasn't the least bit interested in pampering or fearing him.

He grinned at Rafael, whose visage darkened.

# CHAPTER FIVE

A WEEK LATER, nearing evening, Yaniv's travel-weary group approached the Armenta hacienda. He waved at his vaqueros as they split off from the family group to take the wagons and livestock to the barns and corrals. Rafael accompanied them, his defiance a pall over the gathering. Yaniv frowned after his brother. He'd better not bring trouble for them during their stay with the Armentas.

No matter how closely he'd watched his hermano, Rafael continued to plague Maya. As the trip progressed, his brother became more jovial and confident, while Maya became more withdrawn and quieter. Yaniv couldn't help wondering if Rafael sought her out more than he or Helida knew.

Clouds hovered overhead and cooled the weather, a welcome respite from the warmth of the previous two days. The scent of fresh tortillas cooking wafted in the air. The bark of a dog and the shouts of children had his sister and her children peering from the back of the wagon in front of him. Yaniv relaxed. His hermana and her niños deserved a break from traveling and would welcome a few days with friends.

"This is the Armenta hacienda?"

Maya's soft voice surprised him. He'd been so caught up in making sure everything proceeded as planned, he hadn't noticed her drawing alongside him on the sorrel mare. She'd become adept at riding in the past week. She sat with confidence in the saddle, which told him the soreness of the first days had faded to simple tiredness from the long hours. Still, the shadows under her eyes and the hollowness of her cheeks worried him.

"This is their hacienda. A beautiful place." He studied her as she took in the expansive house, bordered on the front with bright flowers.

"On the way here, I remembered Ernesto begged for a special horse, but my father couldn't afford one. I think he might have wanted one of these horses." Her mouth thinned, and she gripped the reins with a ferocity that made the mare dance to the side.

Yaniv longed to comfort her. Surely her mother regretted marrying such a despicable man as Bruno. But a widow with a young child had few options. Bruno might be charming when he wanted to be.

Yaniv almost snorted at the thought. Why hadn't Maya's mother gone to one of the missions to seek help?

"The Armentas' *caballos* are the best. The little sorrel you are riding came from here." Yaniv smiled at her startled expression. "She was too small for breeding, and my father wanted a gentle animal to teach the niños to ride. Don Armenta threw her in as a bonus when we bought our last *manada de caballos*, our herd of horses, from him. We didn't realize how much she would sweeten the deal."

Maya patted the mare's neck. "She has been a good mount, but I feel bad for stealing her from the children."

"On the way home, the niños can have her back."

Maya's eyes widened as she met his gaze. A hint of fear thinned her lips. The smudge of dirt high on her cheek made her resemble one of his more precocious nieces. He tugged off his glove and leaned down to wipe the dirt away. She shivered under his touch.

"Don't worry. I only meant you are becoming such an accomplished horsewoman it is time for you to have a better horse." At the joy and relief that lit her face, his chest expanded. He could stay here for days staring at her, memorizing each of her expressions.

"Yaniv. Welcome!" Lucio Armenta strode toward him, his spurs jangling with each step. His hat sat back on his head and a smile creased his face. "Come in the house. We have rooms prepared and bathwater heating. I know what it is like to travel for days with such a troop."

Yaniv swung down from his horse and embraced his long-time friend. "Thank you." He turned to help Maya down, but Rafael had returned and had his hands on her waist to lift her down. Maya leaned away. The mare snorted. Rafael snatched Maya from the saddle before she could protest.

She shoved against Rafael's chest. He grinned but released her. She stumbled back, and Yaniv caught her. He wanted to slip his arm around her and pull her close to his side. Instead, he stepped between her and his brother. "Go see that our men and animals are settled. We talked about this earlier today." He fought to keep his temper in check.

"I came to fetch your horses. And to help Maya." Rafael leaned down to snatch the sorrel's reins.

Yaniv caught his brother's muttered "slave girl" before he straightened and turned away. He almost made him come back and apologize, but the look on Maya's face stopped his tongue. She wouldn't want Lucio to know her shame. He put his hand between her shoulder blades, pasted on a smile, and turned to his friend.

"Lucio, this is Maya Garza." He kept his hand on Maya's back as he urged her forward.

Lucio's eyebrows lifted. "Bruno Cruz's daughter?"

"Stepdaughter." Maya corrected, then crossed her arms over her middle.

"I remember you as a little waif with big eyes, bringing drinks when your stepfather asked for them." Lucio took Maya's hand and brushed a kiss across the back.

She blushed.

Yaniv could feel her tension against his palm.

"What brings you here with the Madrigal clan?" Lucio released her hand. "Surely Bruno didn't send you to buy horses from us." He tilted his head.

"She...she's...." Yaniv couldn't think of what to say. He couldn't say he'd bought her from her father. He should have planned for this. Of course questions would be asked.

"I have been helping Helida with her baby. Traveling with children can be difficult." Maya's simple words held truth. She *had* been a lot of help to his sister.

Of course, once the baby had recovered from the fever, Maya had spent a lot of time trying to help him. She learned to care for her horse. Offered to get his horse ready in the morning and put her up at night. She brought his food and offered to wash his clothes the night they camped beside water.

In fact, she'd been helping him far more than she'd taken care of Helida's niños.

"When my sisters-in-law travel to the coast with my brothers, they always take along someone to help with the children." Lucio nodded to Maya. "I'm glad you were there for Helida. Would you like to go on inside with the women?" He gestured toward the hacienda.

Helida stepped outside and called to them. "Maya, come in. Let Yaniv and Lucio talk horses." She smiled and motioned with her hand. "I need some help."

Maya glanced toward the barn before she stepped away from Yaniv. He followed her gaze and noted Rafael standing in the open barn doors watching them. How was he to keep the scoundrel from bothering her?

She walked toward the house, moving with an innate grace, her back straight, head held high. He'd come to recognize this as her posture when she was unsure. Clearly, she didn't like Rafael watching her.

"Come." Lucio clapped him on the back. "I will show you the horses we have set aside for you. Some of the finest stock you have ever seen." His cocky grin made Yaniv smile.

"If they aren't what you're looking for, we can ride out and look at the other herds tomorrow." Lucio glanced at him as they strode toward the barn and corrals. "Besides, I want to hear more about Maya and why she is with you. And what is between you and Rafael? There must be more to the story."

Yaniv had much more he could tell. But should he?

MAYA HELD the towel open as Helida placed her wiggling baby on the cloth and shook the excess water from her hands. Maya flipped the towel around Ana and patted the little girl dry.

"I don't know how I manage to get wetter than Ana when I give her a bath." Helida shook the folds of her skirt, where dark stains had made interesting patterns in the cloth. "I'm glad I waited for my bath until she was clean. Can you watch her while I bathe?"

Ana grabbed a strand of Maya's still damp hair and twisted it in her chubby fist. "Yes, I'll get her dressed and keep her in the room they gave me." She actually had her own room! She couldn't ever remember having one of her own. Her mother had her stay with the younger children so she could get up in the night and take care of the boys. She didn't have a sister, so caring for a girl baby was different and fun. And having time to herself was a luxury she had dreamed of but never expected to have.

"There you go, niña." Maya adjusted the gown on the baby and smoothed down her dark hair. Ana waved her fists, pursed her mouth, and cooed like a mourning dove. Maya smiled and tickled her tiny feet before slipping booties on her.

Ana became fascinated with the ties, swinging her feet in the air and trying to grab the strings. Maya chuckled. Maybe someday she could marry and have a chubby little baby who would be happy and fun. That would be much more pleasant than caring for her stepbrothers, who were spoiled and allowed to terrorize her. She had tried to love them. She truly had. But they hadn't made it easy.

"There's my girl." Helida came in the room combing her long hair with a tortoise-shell comb. Her honey-colored skin gleamed from her bath. She was so pretty, and her husband, Tino, doted on her. Maya had never seen a man love his wife like Tino did Helida. Helida missed him because he had taken most of the supply wagons to their home while she and her children came to visit the Armentas.

Watching them together sowed a seed of longing in Maya's heart. Perhaps she would meet a man who would love her in this way. Yet how would she know? So many men professed love but treated their wives poorly. Yaniv's kind eyes came to mind. Her face warmed. Would he be like Tino?

Of course he would. He would treasure whomever he married, and his wife would be blessed to have him as a husband.

She shivered as Rafael came to mind. She didn't want to cause any more friction between the brothers. She didn't tell Yaniv about the times she'd awakened in the night to find Rafael watching her. The first time, she shrieked loud enough to wake Helida. Rafael disappeared, and Maya had said she'd had a nightmare. Not far from the truth. She had slept little since then.

"You are so serious." Helida's words jarred her from her reverie. "What are you thinking about? Do you miss your madre?"

"No." Maya shook her head, then reconsidered. "Yes, some. I don't miss my brothers or stepfather. I am glad to be here."

Helida finished her hair and placed the comb on the stand next to a washbasin. Ana rolled her chubby body to the side in an effort to turn over. Helida laughed at her failed attempt. "Silly niña." She tickled Ana's stomach, and the baby chortled.

Without looking up at Maya, Helida asked, "Why did your stepfather...?"

Maya could see the darkening blush stain Helida's cheeks. She knew what Yaniv's sister asked.

Did she have an answer? Probably.

Did she want to share the story? Maybe it was time.

"Bruno always resented me because I am not his child. He wanted my madre to send me to live with her family, but she refused." She swallowed against a tightening throat. "I think that is the only time she stood up to him. He treated me like a servant. I didn't have the same privileges his sons did. Instead, I served them all." Tears burned Maya's eyes.

"But something must have happened for him to decide to offer you for sale." Helida sat with her back to the wall and lifted Ana to her lap to nurse.

"He's a trader. He isn't very good, I think. Then one of his best ships was lost at sea, and his business collapsed." Maya shuddered at the memory of Bruno's rage.

"For some time, Rafael has been coming to visit and paid unwanted attention to me. I tried to avoid him." She closed her eyes.

"I think Rafael and my step-brother, Ernesto, convinced Bruno to … to …." She couldn't say the rest. If only she'd never met Rafael. Or if he hadn't befriended Ernesto.

But no. Then she wouldn't have met Yaniv, would she? That thought saddened her more than anything.

"I am sorry, Maya." Helida held the baby close and squeezed Maya's arm.

At the comforting gesture, Maya's eyes burned. No one had ever shown her kindness until this past week. Not even her mother.

"You are welcome to stay with us." Helida shifted a sleepy Ana to the other breast. "We have plenty of room at our hacienda and plenty for you to do."

Maya pressed her hand to her chest. Her heart felt full to bursting.

"Thank you. I appreciate you more than I can say. Now I must go see if I can help Yaniv." She put her palm on the floor to stand.

"Why do you need to help him?" Helida tilted her head to the side.

Maya's face heated. "I am trying to pay him back for what he did for me. I owe him so much."

"Pay him back? For what?"

"He bought me, and he set me free." She bit her lip to keep from crying.

"Maya." Helida leaned forward to clasp Maya's hand. "He gave you the *gift* of freedom. He doesn't expect you to pay him anything."

"But he spent so much. I heard him tell you he would not be able to purchase the horse he wanted because of buying me. I am not worth what he gave for me."

"Of course you are. It was a price he gladly paid." Helida held tight to her hand even when she tried to pull away. "If a person gives you a gift and you try to pay them back, then it is no longer a gift. You are as much as throwing the gift back in his face."

Her words froze Maya in place. Was her attempt to repay Yaniv really like a slap in his face? She hadn't meant to do that. Yet how could she not want to help him?

"Do you understand the meaning of true freedom, Maya?"

Maya frowned. "Of course. You don't have to serve anyone or do anything you don't want to do."

"And is that true for you now?" Helida's half-smile said she already knew the answer. "Everything you do right now is something you want to do?"

"Maybe not everything."

Helida sat back, releasing Maya's hand. "There is only one kind of true freedom. That is found in our Savior Jesus Christ. He bought you with His blood. Paid the price for you. And He gives you spiritual freedom––a gift that is beyond any other."

Her new friend's words sank deep. Maya leaped to her feet. She had to get away, to think. She had to find peace and understanding.

# CHAPTER SIX

EXHAUSTION TUGGED at Yaniv's limbs as he rested his arms on the corral rails and watched a vaquero working with a horse as black as midnight. The animal shook his head, his mane rippling like ocean waves. He snorted at the vaquero, dancing to one side as the man tried to mount.

This spirited horse would never do for Maya.

He sighed, letting the breath ease out so Lucio wouldn't hear. Why couldn't he get Maya out of his head? No matter how much distance separated them, he could hear her voice, recall the glints of gold in her hair, and see the saucy tilt of her chin when she felt challenged by someone. She hadn't just gotten under his skin. He feared she'd dug deep into his heart.

What should he do? And did he want to do anything?

Across the corral, a burst of laughter drew his attention. Rafael. Of course. Flirting with one of the Armenta servants. This woman had none of Maya's innocence. She used her wiles to entice and charm every man around her. He'd heard stories about her.

Stories he wouldn't repeat. Why did Lucio allow her to work here when she was such a disruptive influence?

"It seems your brother is entranced by Rosalinda." Lucio frowned as he leaned on the fence next to Yaniv. "She flirts with every man who comes within range. She even tried to flirt with my father."

"Don Armenta?" Yaniv couldn't hide his shock. The don was well known for his harsh demeanor. The other dons respected him, but few were his friends. He'd never heard of the man having anything to do with a woman. Not since his wife died after being gored by a bull.

"Yep. That would have been the shortest flirtation in history." Lucio shook his head and gave a low laugh. "Still, Rosalinda doesn't give up."

"Rafael is too easily influenced." Yaniv didn't want to offend his friend, but he needed to protect his brother from this wayward woman. Then again, maybe this woman would distract Rafael from pursuing Maya.

Lucio faced Yaniv. "Rafael is *un hombre*, not a niño. He can make his own decisions, mi amigo."

"But he makes terrible choices. He is my responsibility. My madre and my hermanas have spoiled him until he feels he can have anything he wants. I must make him see otherwise."

"Why?"

He stared at Lucio. Why *did* he have to watch over everyone? Why had his padre put him in charge of the familia? His vigilance and control had rewarded him with a stomach that burned enough to keep him awake at night and exhaustion that dogged him every day.

"Because it is expected of me." Yaniv felt the weight of those expectations every day. He didn't want to disappoint his familia—or his God.

Lucio turned back to study the black stallion as the animal crow-hopped around the corral in a half-hearted attempt to shake off the vaquero.

"When my hermana was kidnapped by bandoleros—" Not looking at Yaniv, Lucio spoke in a soft tone, almost as if what he shared carried too much emotion. "—I did everything I could. I felt responsible even though I wasn't the one who made the choice to ride in dangerous territory. I wanted to save Yoana and Tía Leya. I couldn't. I later realized I was trying to do my job … and God's, too.

"One morning the padre spoke in chapel about God being our protector. I learned that God has asked me to do what I can for my familia, but there comes a time when I must place them in His hands. 'When my heart is overwhelmed; lead me to the rock that is higher than I.' That verse of Holy Scripture stuck in my head."

Yaniv's breath caught in his chest. Had he been usurping God's authority? Should he let go of Rafael and trust him to God? The thought made his stomach clench—but why? Did he not trust God? Could he simply ignore his brother's dishonorable actions? No. But he could give God space to work.

"I understand." Lucio grinned and clapped him on the shoulder. "It is very hard to let go. Think on it. For now, let's talk horses and then go get something to eat."

The air was filled with the smell of meat roasting and tortillas cooking. Yaniv's stomach rumbled. "Food does sound good." He pushed away from the railing, giving one last, longing look at the feisty stallion.

Lucio led him to one of the closest pastures. A herd of horses grazed not far from the fence. Yaniv counted a dozen, all fine specimens. Their coats gleamed in the setting sun.

A tall bay lifted her head and whickered. The mare meandered toward them, the rest of the herd at her heels. Yaniv enjoyed their grace and clean lines.

Lucio glanced at Yaniv. "Your message said you wanted eight to ten head, but I brought up extra for you to choose from. These are some of our best mares. Did you want to look at any stallions? That black––" Lucio nodded his head back toward the corral. "––isn't for sale, but we have others."

Yaniv smiled. "We have all the stallions we need, although if the black were for sale, I would be tempted." He couldn't keep the longing from his tone as he glanced over his shoulder. With a sigh, he turned back to his friend. "I would like mares to grow our herd. Maybe a couple of geldings, too. Do you happen to have a gelding that is a little older and fairly tame? One that would be good for a lady who isn't very experienced at riding?"

Eyes glinting with a wily look, Lucio grinned at him. "I thought I detected an interest in a certain señorita."

"I'm helping her out." Yaniv scratched the bay's neck as she came close enough to sniff at his shoulder. He related to Lucio the events that transpired in Los Angeles.

Outrage stormed across Lucio's face. "Bruno sold his own daughter?" His eyes narrowed. Yaniv had no doubt that if Bruno stood in front of Lucio, his friend would take a swing at the man, just as he'd been tempted to do when he saw Maya on that table.

"No wonder you feel so protective." The bay moved to Lucio, and he rested his forehead against the animal's cheek. She nibbled the collar of his shirt. He laughed and pushed her away.

"This is the love interest I have. Only mares flirt with me." He grinned at Yaniv. "Tell me about this young woman. Maya. What is she like?"

"She is so eager to please and help everyone."

"That is a good trait." Lucio pushed away one horse, only to have another take its place. "Don't you think?"

"True." Yaniv hesitated. How should he voice his concerns? "I'm not sure she is eager to please because she wants to. I think she feels she owes me, even though I told her she is free to do as she wishes. I wasn't going to bring her with me, but she pled with me to come."

"She trusts you."

Yaniv shook his head. "I think she didn't have anywhere else to go."

"And how do you feel about this señorita? If you are considering a horse for her to ride, your feelings must go beyond protection. Am I right?"

His face warmed under Lucio's steady gaze. "She follows me wherever I go. All the time. Not physically, but in my thoughts, my dreams, she is there. I can't quit thinking about her." He pushed his toe against the fencepost. The bay mare nipped at his hat, catching it in her teeth. He pushed her away with a slap on her neck. She snorted her indignation.

"I know I need to put my family responsibilities ahead of these emotions, but this woman has gotten under my skin."

Lucio's laugh rang out. "Well, my friend, I would say you are well on your way to finding *una esposa*, a wife. At your old age, you need someone sweet and young to care for you."

Yaniv knew his compadre spoke in jest. Still, marriage? His madre tried often to find a señorita he would want to wed, but no one had caught his attention...until Maya. Was it her innocence? Her love of Ana? He didn't know. He only knew it was real.

He heard a sound and glanced around to see Rafael glaring at him as if he'd heard every word.

And thought.

THE GARDEN PLANTS blurred as Maya wove her way along the paths. Helida couldn't be right. She couldn't. All her life, Maya wanted freedom. Freedom from her stepfather's cruelty. Freedom from her stepsiblings' constant derision. Freedom to be herself.

As if she even knew who that was...or could be.

As a niña, she'd dreamed of a prince saving her from the life she lived, but that dream died long ago. No one cared about her.

No one.

Her toe hit the edge of a bench that hid in the shade of a tree, and she sank down on the sheltered seat. The scent of jasmine hung in the air. Birds twittered. Bees buzzed. She swiped at her eyes, refusing to cry. How would that help anyway?

"Are you all right?"

The soft voice startled her. Maya gasped and swung around, her back against the armrest of the bench. At the other end, amid drooping branches, sat a woman. Her mantilla hung forward to cover her features. On her lap rested a book. Her finger pressed against a page as if she'd paused in her reading when Maya stumbled into her sanctuary.

"I'm sorry. I didn't see you here. I will leave." Maya tried to stand, but her skirt caught in the ironwork.

"Please don't leave. I would love some company." The woman's soft voice carried a soothing quality that lulled Maya's skittering pulse and turbulent emotions. "My name is Leya. Did you come with the Madrigals?" Leya brushed the edge of her mantilla to the side.

Maya caught a glimpse of brown eyes filled with compassion and curiosity. "I...yes." She wiped the moisture from her cheek with the back of her hand and sniffed, hoping her nose wouldn't drip. She hadn't brought a handkerchief with her. "I'm Maya."

"Maya." Leya hummed a thoughtful sound. "I don't recall your name being mentioned with the Madrigals before. Perhaps you are a new wife to Rafael or Yaniv."

*"No."* Maya wanted to bite her tongue for the sharpness of her tone. The horror at the image of being a señora to Rafael made her shudder. However, the thought of being married to Yaniv had an appeal she shouldn't consider. He was far above her station.

She enjoyed doing things for him, helping him in little unexpected ways. But after talking with Helida, she wasn't sure how to act around him anymore. Maybe she should have stayed in Los Angeles, even if Bruno sold her again.

"Are you helping Helida with her baby then? A nursemaid?" Leya asked.

"Yes." Maya grasped at the notion. She *had* helped on the way here. That might not be the whole truth, but it was true enough. Her conscience nibbled at her mind. "That is not the only reason I am traveling with them, but I did help with Ana."

She couldn't seem to stop her tongue. Without looking at Leya, she rested back against the bench and told the whole sordid story. When she finished by telling Leya what Helida said to her and how confused she'd become, the older woman sat silent for a long time.

Had she fallen asleep?

If the garden and the hidden alcove hadn't been so peaceful, Maya might have slipped away and left the woman to her nap. After several minutes, she decided to leave and rose from the bench.

"Maya."

She clapped a hand to her chest, her heart galloping.

"Yes?"

"Stay a minute longer, please. I'd like to talk to you about what Helida said. True freedom. Do you understand what she meant?" She gently clasped Maya's hand.

Maya listened as the older woman talked about her own horrific experiences. Kidnapped at about the same age Maya was now. Abused by outlaws. Scarred so badly she had to stay hidden away and would never know a man's love.

How could a man ever treat such a woman that way? How could Leya survive and be so sweet?

Maya's heart burned. If those who hurt this woman had not been punished, she wanted to find them and make them sorry they'd ever been born!

Leya told how she had given her heart to God, and He'd given her a gift more precious than an unscarred face. Maya's breath caught. Did God have something special for her too? Did He love her that much? Could He help her forgive?

"You see, Maya, when you give yourself to Jesus and ask Him to guide you through life, He gives your soul a freedom that is unavailable any other way. His peace will surround you in terrible times. Don't just believe there is a God. Know Him. Trust Him, Maya."

As they prayed together, warmth flooded through Maya. Peace and the beginning of understanding filled her, causing her to weep. She had known of God and His son, Jesus, but never like this. She wanted to jump up. To shout for joy. To tell everyone about the goodness of God.

"You must pray about what God wants you to do. I am sure you would be welcome to stay here and work on the rancho. If you ask, He will show you." Leya squeezed her hands and stood. "Now, I must get inside and see to the evening meal. I have enjoyed our talk, Maya."

"Thank you." Maya stood and brushed another tear from her cheek. This time, a tear of joy.

She thought about the offer Leya made. To stay here at this lovely hacienda. She could be happy here. She could work in the kitchen or help with the household chores. She could even help with the children.

"God, show me exactly what you want me to do." She breathed the prayer as she stepped from the garden and saw the corrals ahead of her. Beyond the barn, a few horses milled by a fence.

Her footsteps were resolute as she crossed the open ground. She would ask Lucio if they had a job for her here. Then she would not be a burden to the Madrigal family. She would be free of Rafael.

And she would not be tempted to keep doing things for Yaniv.

Her resolve held firm—until the two men at the fence turned to face her.

Lucio...and Yaniv.

Her steps faltered. His gaze stole her breath. The voice of God whispered across her heart, and Maya knew.

She had to stay with him. To help him however she could. Not to repay him, but because, God help her...

She loved him.

# CHAPTER SEVEN

YANIV COULDN'T TAKE his eyes off Maya. She had none of the seductive sway adopted by so many women or the sensual allure they used to attract men. But her beauty rivaled that of any woman he'd ever met. She shone with innocence and down-to-earth goodness.

He glanced at Lucio, saw the masculine appreciation in his friend's expression. An unfamiliar emotion burned in the pit of Yaniv's stomach. Jealousy? He tamped down the urge to step between Maya and Lucio.

He noted the moment her steps faltered. He turned to look, as did Lucio. On the far side of the corral, Rafael grinned at Maya. His expression held the predatory gleam of a beast eyeing its prey. Though Rafael had Rosalinda in his arms, that didn't deter him from watching Maya. Yaniv grunted as Rafael turned and walked away with the beautiful Rosalinda.

Lucio stared after them, jaw clenched.

Yaniv and his friend turned back around. Maya continued toward them, hers steps not as confident. He smiled as she drew close. *Smiled.*

He hadn't smiled in a long time, but the lightness inside him wouldn't be denied. The tension in her expression eased. Her rounded cheeks dimpled as she returned the smile. The sparkle in her eyes stole his breath.

*His.*

He wanted her to be his.

"Señorita Garza." Lucio took Maya's hand and bent to brush a kiss against the back, just above her fingers, as he had upon meeting her. "You look refreshed. Again, welcome to the Armenta hacienda."

Yaniv almost ripped her hand from Lucio's. A growl wormed its way up his throat, and he stuffed the sound back down. Lucio was his friend. Not one of the men back in the cantina. Not some lowlife. His friend.

"Thank you." Pink tinged Maya's cheeks as she withdrew her hand from Lucio's grip. "You have a beautiful home. Are these some of the famous Armenta horses?"

"They are." Lucio swept his hand toward the fenced pasture as he straightened. "Yaniv is trying to choose some mares but seems to be having trouble. A common problem among those who come to buy our stock."

"I can see why." Maya stepped past them to the fence and held out her hand to the closest mare. The horse chuffed a breath against her palm. Maya's delighted laugh made Yaniv's heart soar. Oh, to hear her laugh more often.

"My eye isn't trained to see the differences in horses, but yours look superb."

Yaniv watched her step closer to the fence, where the mares grouped around to greet her. Amazing how comfortable she'd become among these animals in such a short time. She had a way with them. All of his vaqueros talked about her.

"I spoke to Lucio about acquiring a different mount for you." He almost smiled at the startled look on her face as she whirled around.

"I...I..." She swallowed hard. Her hands clenched into fists. The joy of moments before faded from her countenance. "I have no money to pay for such a fine animal." She lowered her gaze as her color darkened.

Yaniv's teeth squeaked as he gritted them. He'd spoken without thinking. Again. "I'm sorry." Words failed him at the misery in her eyes. He hadn't meant to embarrass her or to suggest she would have to pay for the animal. He hadn't realized how awkward this would be. He only wanted to do something nice for her.

"Perhaps you don't understand." Lucio's light tone told Yaniv his friend also felt the unease of the moment. "Yaniv will purchase the horse with the others. We have some gentler stock that will work well for you as you gain skill. He can use the animal on his ranch for others who need a gentle mount. This will free up the *caballito* for the children."

"But I don't..."

"Don't say it." Yaniv held up his hand. "You have helped my sister with Ana. You have helped with the cooking and a myriad of other chores around the camp. You have learned to take care of the horses and have been kind to every person there. Someone of your character is a treasure and worth the investment of a horse."

The flush in her face deepened. She twisted her hands together in front of her.

She might not realize that, coming from him, what he said was high praise indeed, but Lucio did. His raised eyebrows made Yaniv want to squirm like a young schoolboy caught teasing a girl he was sweet on.

Lucio smiled at Yaniv. "If you have a few minutes to come to the barn, I have the perfect horse in mind." He motioned to the large building not far away. "We have a mare who recently lost her foal. This is the third time she has been unable to carry a foal to term. We have talked of getting rid of her, and while she wouldn't be good for you as breeding stock, she is a calm horse and would make a good mount for the señorita."

They headed for the building, and Yaniv held out his arm for Maya so she wouldn't stumble on the uneven ground. He could feel the imprint of her small fingers through his shirtsleeve. If only the walk were longer––or he had more of an excuse to touch her.

His mind fumbled for something to say. A way to distract his thoughts from Maya. "How old is this mare?" He didn't want to bring home a mare that could not breed. Did he?

"She is seven years. She gave birth twice but has lost every foal since then." Lucio led them into the musty warmth of the barn. The scent of hay and manure surrounded them. The buzz of flies sounded a constant drone. "She is still recovering from losing her last foal. She's normally calm but has been distressed."

Even though Maya hadn't grown up around horses, or riding them anyway, she didn't seem offended at the smell. The Armentas kept their barn clean, but the day was warm, so the odor could be overwhelming. As they followed Lucio down the center aisle, Yaniv wanted to weave his fingers with Maya's. Just to touch her.

As if she understood his thoughts, she let her hand slip down to her side. The lack of physical connection left him bereft.

"Here she is." Lucio motioned for them to join him at a stall. A horse nickered and shuffled to the door. She didn't seem to have much energy. Maybe from being cooped up. The palomino thrust her nose over the edge of the door, stretching out toward Maya, whose eyes glimmered her delight as she stroked the mare's nose.

"Let me bring her out so you can see her. She needs some fresh air anyway." Lucio lifted a rope from the wall and looped it around the horse's neck and nose in deft movements.

Yaniv touched Maya's shoulder. "Let's move back so he can open the stall."

Lucio led the mare out, and they followed at a discreet distance.

Maya gasped. "Look how her coat catches the sunshine. It looks like polished gold."

The palomino flung her head up, white showing around her eyes. Her sides heaved as she let out a loud neigh. She danced around Lucio, her frantic gaze tracking back to the barn. Yaniv pulled Maya close.

Why would Lucio want him to buy a crazed horse for Maya?

He opened his mouth to ask when a medium-sized dog trotted from the barn. The mare nickered again, more softly this time. The dog meandered closer to her and sat down. She lowered her head to sniff him, all traces of her panic fading.

"Ramón." Lucio's mouth set in a grim line. Yaniv heard the stomp of footfalls and turned to see a vaquero rounding the side of the building. Before he could say a word, Lucio spoke. "Why is this cur still here? I told you to get rid of him."

Ramón shrugged. "One of the boys wanted to try to tame him. I thought I'd let him have a go since every time we attempted to remove him, the mare would go crazy."

"Did he have any success?" Lucio almost spat out the question.

"No. The mutt still won't let anyone touch him."

"Then I want him gone. He's a danger with the children around. I don't care how much he calms the mare. She'll get used to not having him." Lucio drew in a deep breath and looked at Yaniv. His mouth quirked.

Yaniv started. When had he put his arm around Maya? He had her crushed against his side in a most inappropriate manner. He eased his grip and she stepped away. Not far though, which comforted him. Maybe she hadn't minded him holding her close.

"Get your gun. No. Wait." Lucio glanced at Maya. Her attention stayed on the dog and the mare.

He gave Yaniv a look as if to ask him to take her away, but before he could move, Maya took a step, and then another, toward the dog. Yaniv tensed

If the cur so much moved an inch...

Maya knelt in the dirt. The dog cowered beside the mare, lips pulled back to show a glimpse of sharp canines.

He growled.

THE FILTHY DOG could have been all brown, or maybe a mottled cream and brown. Maya wasn't sure because his coat had so much manure and straw ground in. He looked like a walking dirt clod.

With teeth.

And warm brown eyes that showed a hint of hope. Maya's heart went out to this mutt so much like her and considered worthless. Something to be discarded.

Why did life have to be so hard?

"Hey, *chico*." She eased her hand toward the dog, fingers outstretched, palm up.

"Maya, get back. He will bite you."

Despite the tension in the air, she ignored Lucio's warning. Something about this pathetic creature drew her. She had to give him a chance before they killed him.

The rumble in the dog's chest softened. He stretched his nose toward her hand. The mare leaned her head down to sniff her friend, as if encouraging him. The dog's cool nose touched Maya's fingertips. She held her breath.

His pink tongue licked her hand. Then he jerked back.

Had this dog been beaten? Anger burned inside her at the thought.

"*Está bien.*" She crooned as he began to ease his nose close once again. This time when he licked her, he didn't jerk away but allowed her to run her thumb over his muzzle. He closed his eyes, let his snout rest in her open palm, and sighed.

Tears stung Maya's eyes. How she longed for the same thing. A comforting caress from someone who cared. Had Yaniv's touch been that of someone who cared, or simply his protective nature?

"I don't believe this." Ramón's eyes were wide. "Several of the hands have tried to touch him. He bit Gilberto for coming too close."

Maya sank back onto a patch of grass. The dog belly-crawled

toward her to lean his filthy body against her legs. Part of her cringed at the thought of petting him without giving him a bath first, but she understood. He needed the comfort right now.

She stroked his head. His muzzle. His ears.

"Looks like we will take the horse and the dog for Maya." Yaniv sounded amused.

She glanced up at him, startled that he would do something so generous and kind. She should have known. He'd been kind to her, an outcast, from the very first.

"Thank you." She ducked her head to keep him from seeing the tears that threatened to fall. She ignored the men as she talked in low tones to the creature huddled against her. "I think I will call you Dante because you have endured, even when they wanted to be rid of you."

Dante lifted his muzzle and licked her cheek.

A loud bell clanged from the nearby house. On cue, her stomach rumbled, a reminder she hadn't eaten in hours. Dante growled low, more a rumble she felt than a sound she heard. She looked up to see Yaniv extending his hand toward her.

"Let me help you up, and we'll go for our meal." He didn't seem perturbed with her as Bruno would have been. Of course, Bruno would have dragged Dante away and killed him while she watched. He would have laughed at her horror. He'd done just that to every animal she ever befriended.

"What about Dante?" She patted her new friend, accepted Yaniv's hand, and stood.

"Dante?" Yaniv's mouth quirked in a smile.

Her face heated. "That's what I've named him. He is very strong inside."

Yaniv squeezed her hand while Lucio chuckled and led the mare back toward the barn.

Maya leaned down to pet Dante one more time. He seemed unsure whether to stay with her or follow the horse. She motioned for him to go, and he trudged away.

"In the morning I will give him a bath." She wrinkled her nose at the smell that clung to her clothes.

"*That* will be interesting." Yaniv shook his head. "I'll bet Lucio could sell tickets to the event, and all his vaqueros would pay to watch."

She smiled. She couldn't help it. He was probably right. Dante would not be happy about being dowsed with water and scrubbed. The men would gather and watch as she washed her dog...

The thought brought back the horror in the cantina. She stumbled. Bile burned bitterly at the back of her throat. The dimness. Men crowding close. Hands reaching for her. The stench. The perversion. The hopelessness...

Panic shot through her, and she tried to push it away. Freedom. Leya shared verses about freedom and God's love. She had to cling to that hope. Her hands twisted in her skirts as she fought to hide her fear from Yaniv.

To no avail.

He cupped her elbow. "What is it? What's upset you?"

She wanted to pull away, but that would offend him. He wasn't like Bruno. He wasn't like Rafael. He wasn't like her brothers. He would not destroy what she treasured. Would he?

"I must go wash up." She tugged her arm free and turned away.

Dust puffed up with each step as she hurried across the open dirt toward the hacienda.

"Maya, wait." Yaniv's boots thudded on the earth behind her. He caught her arm and pulled her around. "You can't just run off like that when I ask what is wrong. I can't help you if you don't talk to me."

"It's nothing." What could she say? How could he possibly understand?

"Did I say something wrong? Something to hurt you?"

He stood so close she couldn't think. Part of her wanted to leap away from him, but another part wanted to fall into his arms. Her emotions were all over the place. She didn't know what she wanted anymore.

Yaniv?

*No!*

Thoughts of the way Bruno treated her mother made her insides quiver. She didn't want to live through that with any man. But wouldn't Yaniv be different? Would he be like Helida's Tino? Could she trust him?

"I can't accept your generosity." She blurted the words, and his eyes widened.

"What generosity is that?"

"I can't let you purchase that mare for me. I will ride the children's horse or ride in the wagon. Or I'll walk." She was being unreasonable, but she couldn't help it.

"Why, Maya? I don't understand." His calm tone and tender eyes tore at her defenses.

"I can't stand it again."

"Can't stand what?"

His face blurred through her tears. She knew he was different, but what if he wasn't?

"I can't stand to have another animal die because of me."

# CHAPTER EIGHT

MAYA PULLED AWAY from Yaniv and ran toward the hacienda. She hadn't meant to blurt out the truth. What must he think? She pressed a hand against her stomach, her throat aching. Why had she compared Yaniv to Bruno? They were nothing alike. But how, after all those years of living in that house, could she ever trust any man?

She'd noted all the little torments Bruno inflicted on her mother. He thought he'd been so sly, but Maya saw her mother's fear. Heard terrible sounds in the night. Grieved at the way her mother moved slowly the next day, doing her best not to show her pain.

In the room assigned to her, Maya pulled off her soiled dress and washed in the basin of water left on a stand. Helida had loaned her a dress that was a little longer and bigger around than her own gown, so Maya slid the clean dress on, grateful she could go to dinner not reeking of a horse's stall. She patted a stray strand of hair into place and left her room, not sure where they would gather to eat.

She followed the sound of voices. Her steps slowed. Down the hallway, she could see the door that must lead to the dining area. She stopped. Saw a servant carry a tray into the room. She stepped closer. Remembered the hurt that had flashed in Yaniv's eyes when she'd hurled accusations.

She leaned against the wall, closing her eyes against the onslaught of tears. She would not cry. She straightened. Swiped at her eyes. Slipped through the entry that led to the kitchen. She wasn't truly part of the family. Would the Armentas want to have her at their table when they discovered Yaniv had purchased her at a cantina? Would the servants welcome her in their domain?

No matter what Yaniv said, she was still his slave. Who else knew he'd set her free? Rafael? He still called her a slave. What did the small piece of paper Yaniv had given her mean? What if they accused her of deceiving Yaniv? Of using her wiles to get close to him? What would happen to her then?

One of the Armenta servants came out of the dining room to her left, where she could hear voices and chatter. She smiled at Maya and motioned to the open door. Maya took a step. Hesitated. The girl stopped beside her.

"May I help you?"

"I know the familia is expecting me, but I would rather join you in the kitchen. Would you show me where you have your meals?" She watched uncertainty play across the young girl's face before she glanced toward the kitchen. Her dusky skin and huge eyes gave her the look of a lost waif.

"Yes, follow me."

The girl led the way to a door that opened into a room filled with activity. Maya stopped to take it all in. Even the Ávilas' kitchen had not been this busy. She hadn't realized the Armenta hacienda housed and fed so many.

"Vincenta, who is this? We don't bring guests in here." A heavyset woman who must be the head cook glared at the young girl.

"Please, I asked her to bring me here." Maya stepped up beside Vincenta. "I am a sl...servant for the Madrigals and am uncomfortable eating with the familia."

The cook wiped a drop of sweat from her forehead onto her sleeve. She nodded. Pointed with a long fork dripping some sort of juices. "There's a table through there."

Maya made her way around the edge of the kitchen to another opening that led to a small room. A long table lined with benches almost filled the empty chamber. She sank onto the end bench and glanced around. Where were the other people who ate here?

A few moments later, Vincenta came through carrying a plate piled with food and a cup of water. She set everything in front of Maya and turned to go.

"Wait." The scent of beans and roasted meat made Maya's stomach rumble. "Where are the others? Why is no one else eating?"

Vincenta's head ducked. She folded her hands together in front of her skirt, twisting the material. "We will eat after the familia is finished. And after we have taken food to the men in the bunkhouse. Please go ahead. Don't let your meal get cold."

Maya caught a glimpse of dark eyes through Vincenta's lowered lashes before the girl disappeared back into the kitchen. Her throat tightened. She wouldn't be able to swallow a single bite of her meal. Her chest ached. She rested her forehead on her palm and closed her eyes, her body heavy. One friend. She wanted one friend to talk to. Something she'd never had...

And would never have.

She picked up the tortilla and tore off a small bite. Held the scrap in her fingers as tears pricked her eyes. What would happen to her? Did anyone truly want her?

Footsteps thundered on the wood floor of the kitchen. Not the light patter of the servants' slippered feet. Heavy boots. She looked up through the blur of moisture in her eyes as Yaniv strode into the room. The bit of tortilla dropped to the table.

He stopped, legs spread, hands on his hips. Her heart flipped at his darkened face.

"Why are you in here by yourself?" He shook his head. "You are part of my familia now, Maya. You will eat with us."

His tone softened, as did the hardness of his expression. "Come. You are missed."

She couldn't move. Didn't know what to do. Yaniv crossed to her and slipped his hand under her elbow. His gentle touch lifted her to her feet. She reached for her plate.

"Leave it." He urged her to the door. "There is already a place set for you at our table. We have plenty of food."

The stares of the Armenta servants prickled against her back. She wanted to tell them she was no one special. Just a slave. As such, she would have to do as told. But they wouldn't understand. Why would a slave be asked to join a family meal?

"There you are." Helida's face lit in a smile as Maya and Yaniv entered the dining room. She patted an empty seat beside her. "Come sit with me."

Yaniv led Maya around the long table. Her stomach fluttered. She couldn't breathe. Conversation quieted. Oh, to be in her room and away from those watching her! What were they thinking?

"For those of you who haven't met her, this is Maya. She is traveling with us and will be staying with our family." Yaniv held her chair, then slipped into the seat beside her.

Across the table, Rafael clinked his fork against his plate. She glanced up at him. The slight tilt of his mouth told her where his thoughts strayed. Her appetite fled. She wanted to leave but knew she had to stay.

As soon as Maya's plate was filled, Helida leaned close. "I heard you tamed a wild beast." Her eyes sparkled as she scooped up a bite of meat and beans. "All the men are talking about how you sat with the dog they thought was untamable." Her low chuckle warmed Maya as she worked to keep from looking across the table.

"They won't hurt him, will they?" Maya's breath stuttered in her chest. Should she have stayed at the barn to protect Dante? What if Lucio took this opportunity to get rid of the dog that plagued them? She put her palms against the table edge to push away.

"Stop." Helida's light touch held her in place. "Your dog is safe. Yaniv made sure Lucio's men would leave the animal alone. He told me he would have instructed them to clean the creature, but he wasn't sure they would survive." She gave a low laugh.

Relief swept through her––along with another emotion she couldn't quite figure out. Gratitude? Wonder? She gave a sideways glance at Yaniv and caught him staring at her. Her skin prickled. His sleeve brushed against her arm as he scooped another bite. Her breath caught again, but not in fear.

A foot nudged hers under the table. She tightened her hold on her fork and refused to look at Rafael. She tucked her feet under her chair.

They were finishing their meal when a distant uproar slowed the chatter in the room. Everyone turned toward the door. Shouts.

The clatter of dishes. Maya could see nothing from where she sat. Some of the men surged to their feet. Had bandoleros attacked the rancho? She'd heard of such things but hadn't thought them to be true.

Ramón, the vaquero who'd spoken with Lucio earlier, rushed into the room, a lasso in his hands. He froze, his gaze finding Lucio. The women closest to him plucked out handkerchiefs and covered their noses. Maya leaned forward trying to see what had upset everyone.

*"What* is going on?" Lucio threw down a cloth he'd used to wipe his mouth and rounded the table toward Ramón.

"I'm sorry. We couldn't stop him." Ramón panted as if he'd run all the way from Los Angeles. "I thought he would kill someone. We tried to lasso him, but he's too smart."

"What are you talking about?" Lucio's nostrils widened. He sniffed. Glanced at Yaniv.

Now Maya caught a whiff of what the others were reacting to. The same noxious odor she'd smelled earlier. Yaniv's hand gripped her arm. The horrible smell became stronger. Beside her, Helida gagged into her handkerchief. Across the table, Rafael shoved back, stood, and left the room.

An instant of relief at her tormentor being gone faded, and Maya's stomach swooped. Like she'd fallen off a cliff. Something nudged her elbow. She turned in her chair and looked down into expressive eyes. Dante...

... the noxious.

～

"I THINK PERHAPS WAITING until tomorrow to bathe the dog is

unwise." Yaniv almost couldn't keep from laughing at the greenish tinge on his sister's face. She pressed a cloth to her nose as she stared at the filth dropped on the floor behind them.

"Dante." Maya cupped the dog's face in a touch so tender Yaniv ached. Her gaze had softened, and he knew she'd shut out everyone in the room. What he wouldn't give to have her look at him like that.

"Maya, is there a way we can convince your friend to leave the room?" Lucio and Ramón had come part way down the table behind the chairs. The mutt's low growl halted them. Only Maya seemed unaffected by the dog's threats.

"I'm sorry." Maya pushed back her chair and rose to her feet. "I will take him outside. I can change back into my other dress and bathe him."

Dante lifted to his feet, the rumble of his growl increasing. Yaniv figured his fur would be standing on end if he didn't have so much dirt and manure crusted all over him.

Lucio grimaced. "Ramón, could you get that spare trough and fill it with water?" He stepped back to make way for Maya and the mutt. "Have extra water on hand and some good soap. I think he will need ten baths before he smells decent enough for human company."

Yaniv rubbed a hand across his mouth. Lucio glared at him, but he saw the twitch of his friend's mouth and knew the humor of this moment would spread around the ranch.

"I believe I will find some less respectable clothing and see if I can help Maya." Yaniv nodded to Lucio as he headed for the room he would be sharing with Rafael. He wished he could ask for his own room and for his brother to be elsewhere but would not stoop to such rudeness.

The ladies stood in the hallway, still holding cloths over their noses as servants hurried to sweep up the debris left by Dante's passing and wash away the smell. Or at least try to do so. That stench would not be gone anytime soon. Had the dog rolled in something dead or perhaps slept with something rancid in the stall? How could Maya stand the foul stink? Yet she seemed more concerned with the mutt's wellbeing than any olfactory offense.

By the time Yaniv met Lucio outside, Maya and Dante were waiting as a tub was filled. She had a rope around the dog's neck, and he sat, tail sweeping the ground, leaning toward her as if hearing the most interesting conversation ever. If the beast hadn't been so filthy, the picture of the pair would be charming.

Maya had pinned her braid up in a bun at the back of her neck. He could see the curve of her cheek and the slender line of her neck as she knelt close to Dante. He wanted to see her eyes and the sparkle that would be in those depths. Her deep love for animals touched him. How had she continued to love and trust anything after all she'd been through? Would she be able to apply the same principles to people? He prayed she could heal from those wounds and learn to love again.

He wanted to be part of her healing. And one day, maybe, just maybe, a recipient of her love. *Please, God, touch her heart. Show her Your love so she will know how to love others.* He drew in a deep breath, nearly choking on the acrid air. *If it is Your will, show me favor, and let Maya return the feelings I'm developing for her. Thank you.*

Several ranch hands strode across the yard carrying buckets of water. They poured some in the tub and saved the others for rinsing. Maya stood, lifting the rope, then stopped to frown down at Dante.

She turned toward Yaniv. "Do you think we should wet him down first before putting him in the clean water?"

Her deference to him over Lucio pleased Yaniv more than he wanted to say. "He will take multiple baths to smell better, but if you can even get him to take even one, that will help. See if he will get in the water."

Her smile lit a small fire in his heart. "I've been talking to him. He will do it."

The men backed away, and she led Dante forward. He stretched out his nose to sniff the tub, leaned in, and lapped some water. He lifted his muzzle toward Maya. She gestured with her hand, and he leaped in as if that had been his intention all along.

Beside Yaniv, Lucio grunted his disbelief. The ranch hands stood open-mouthed.

Maya slid to her knees, ignoring the moist dirt that soaked her dress. She used an old pan to dip water and pour it over Dante's head. He shivered, shook his head, and flung brown goo away from him. The men jumped back, making Maya laugh. The tinkling sound floated in the air and seemed to mesmerize the others as much as it did him.

They all were frozen in place, watching the performance.

By the second tub of water, a brown-and-black dog began to emerge. After the third rinse, Maya rubbed Dante with an old rag, and his coat gleamed. He panted, tongue hanging out, eyes fixed on Maya.

Yaniv fought a grin. So he wasn't the only one to adore this señorita. Maybe if he covered himself in filth, she would turn her adoring gaze on him. He almost snorted a laugh.

A loud whinny pierced the quiet night. On sudden alert, Dante jerked toward the barn.

"Almost done." Maya's voice seemed to calm the dog, and he settled back on his haunches.

Lucio smiled at Maya. "I had some of the men clean out the mare's stall and put new straw on the floor. They also put an old blanket in the corner where the dog likes to sleep. Maybe when he's finally clean, he won't go back into the muck."

Maya shot him a look of gratitude. The mare neighed again, this time with a definite note of panic. Dante whined, jerked back, and slipped free of the rope. He shot across the grounds at a dead run.

Lifting her skirt, Maya followed the mutt. Yaniv shook his head at Lucio and headed after her. He caught up to her as she stopped outside the stall door. They both peered over the divider to see Dante sniffing at the clean straw as the mare nudged him with her nose.

"Thank you. This is so nice." Maya's eyes glittered with moisture as the dog turned in circles and sank down on to the blanket.

Oh, if only he could get her to care for him as much as she cared for a miserable beast.

# CHAPTER NINE

THE SWEET SCENT of jasmine drifted through the open window. A shaft of early morning sunlight nudged at Maya's eyelids. She wanted to brush it away and go back to sleep. She'd been up late last night bathing Dante, cleaning up afterward, answering questions about her gift with animals. She'd enjoyed the interest shown her, especially by Yaniv, but at the same time had been uncomfortable. No one ever considered her worthy of notice. She'd hidden her ability with animals for so long out of fear of Bruno's retribution. Even here, in a place that seemed safe, she carried that sense of doom, as if something horrible waited just around the corner.

Did she deserve to be happy?

She rolled to the side to get away from the brightness of the sunbeam. Her muscles screamed. So many new experiences since she left Los Angeles. Good experiences. Challenging experiences. Ones she wanted to forget, and ones she wanted to savor.

The memory of Yaniv kneeling beside her in the muck last night had her pressing her palms to her chest. She could feel the thump of her heart. He'd been so kind to her. So kind to Dante. He didn't raise his voice or belittle her in front of others. He treated her as if her opinion mattered. As if *she* mattered. She blinked away the burn of tears.

Did love happen this fast? Did she truly love Yaniv? Or was she just reacting to the first kind man she'd ever met? What was true love? She didn't think her mother loved the man she'd married. Had she loved Maya's father? What would loving Yaniv be like?

"God, please help me. Show me the truth."

Her whispered plea drifted upward in the quiet of the room. No response. Yesterday, she'd felt God answer her. Maybe He only paid attention at a certain time of the day. Or in a certain place. Should she go pray in the garden?

She slipped from the bed and dressed, splashing water on her face and braiding her hair. On the way out, she grabbed her borrowed *rebozo* and draped it over her shoulders. She met no one in the hallway. Low voices came from the kitchen area as the servants prepared breakfast. She pictured the large stone basins they used to mix the masa for tortillas even as she heard the clang of the cast-iron skillets being heated on the stove.

She left by the side door hoping no one heard her.

Sand crunched beneath her feet as she slipped down the path she'd taken yesterday. A few birds twittered in the tree branches. A rabbit hopped across the path, spotted her, and disappeared in the undergrowth. She smiled as the cottony tail disappeared from view.

The bench she'd sat on yesterday beckoned her. The stillness of the early morning surrounded her as if the garden held its breath, waiting to see what the day would bring. Maya sank down, closed her eyes, and tilted her head back to breathe deeply. The fresh scent of flowers, plants, and earth comforted her. She stayed like that, listening. What would God say to her? Peace stole through her. A peace that spoke of comfort and trust. Spoke that she needn't worry about anything because the One who had her best interests in mind was in control. She smiled.

"It's good to know you're happy to see me."

Her eyes flew open. Rafael stood close, arms crossed over his broad chest. His dark eyes glittered in the morning light, a hunter pleased to finally corner his prey.

Her fingers curled around the edge of the bench as her mind fumbled with her options. The path was too narrow, so she couldn't dart past him. He would snatch her up, and she would never get free. She couldn't go over the back of the bench. The thick growth would be too hard to penetrate, and he would catch her. Panic clawed the back of her throat. Even if she screamed, he would stop her before anyone heard.

"What do you want?" Her taut muscles ached. Her palms grew damp. If she could get him to move to her right, she might have space to flee past him. But how to get him to move?

"You. That's all I've ever wanted. You."

"But I don't want you." She fought for breath through the tightness in her lungs. Maybe...maybe she had a choice. "I'm sorry, but I am not the one for you. Please leave me alone."

She wanted to explain why, but he stepped closer. Leaned down until she couldn't avoid his gaze.

A thin layer of pride faded from his face, leaving something startling there.

Vulnerability.

But the moment passed, and the corner of his mouth lifted. "I know Yaniv is taken with you. I see the way he watches you."

Her pulse leaped.

"But I want you more. I should have been the one to buy you from your father." He captured her chin in his hand. She jerked free.

"From my mother's husband. *Not* my father."

"He is your father by marriage." He grabbed her arm. His fingers dug into the tender flesh, making her wince.

"Let go of me." She had to leave. Just being in this secluded spot with Rafael would ruin any reputation she had left. The realization chilled her. What if they were discovered, and she had to marry Rafael? He would win. She would lose.

*God, please help me. Please.*

Rafael dragged her to her feet. Grabbed her other arm. Lifted her until her toes didn't even touch the path.

She shoved against his chest. Fought for breath and the strength to break free, but to no avail. He clasped her to him, his mouth perilously close to hers. She turned her head to avoid his kiss.

A brown blur raced toward them. *Dante!*

The dog snarled and leaped at Rafael. Rafael yelped when the dog's teeth sank in his arm. As he stepped back, he lost his footing and stumbled. His grip loosened as he tumbled to the ground, the growling dog on top of him.

Maya jerked free as she fell, leaped up, and ran for the house. Harsh breaths scraped up and down her throat. Spots danced in front of her eyes. She didn't dare slow down. Rafael would catch her before she reached the safety of her room. But Dante. What if

Rafael hurt her dog? She slid to a stop by the house and let out a low whistle. Dante raced down the path toward her.

The door handle slipped in the sweat of her palms. Footsteps pounded closer on the path. A high, keening sound rushed past her, and she realized the noise came from her. The latch came free. The door opened, and she stumbled inside. Dante darted past her as she slammed the door.

Her legs trembled, but she didn't dare stop. What if he came through the door after her? He'd been so determined. So forceful. So maniacal. Dante whined. She snapped her fingers for him to follow her.

She raced around the corner, her attention focused back on the door handle. She slammed into someone. Heard the grunt. Felt the arms come around her. Panic filled her again. Had Rafael come in a different way? She struggled, tried to scream. The arms tightened.

"Maya. Maya! ¿Qué pasa? What is wrong?"

"Let her go!" Rafael's shout came from behind her, bursting through the haze of panic.

Dante growled.

Maya froze. If Rafael stood behind her... The touch. The scent. A wave of relief weakened her shaky legs, and she sagged against Yaniv.

"She is mine, Yaniv." Rafael's tone lowered, filled with a dangerous rage. "You stole her from me, and I want her back."

Yaniv didn't loosen his hold.

"Yaniv." Helida's light perfume washed over Maya as she swept past. "Yaniv, will you please take Maya to my room? The baby is waking up, so Maya can change and bathe her."

Helida turned to Rafael. "I would like to go out in the garden for a stroll before breakfast. Accompany me." Her tone brooked no argument.

Rafael growled low in his throat, a sound similar to Dante's. His heavy footsteps faded along with Helida's lighter steps.

"Come, Maya. You're shaking like a leaf." Yaniv's hold tightened for just a moment before he released her.

She couldn't look at him. After her run through the garden, plus the tears she couldn't stop, she must look a mess. Did he despise her for the strife she'd caused between him and his brother?

Yaniv's thumbs brushed across her cheeks, wiping away the moisture. He cupped her chin and lifted it until she could see his face. His gaze wasn't angry. He smiled. A slight lifting of the lips, but enough to tell her he didn't blame her.

"I'm sorry he won't listen to reason. I don't think Rafael has ever been denied anything in his life, especially not by a woman. My mother and sisters have indulged his every whim." He traced the curve of her lower lip with his thumb. "I will see that he never bothers you again." His eyes glittered, and she shivered, thinking about what he intended to do to Rafael.

He leaned closer. She could feel his breath on her cheek—

*No!* Her heart pounded. She couldn't breathe. She jerked back.

Hurt flashed in Yaniv's eyes, gone so fast she almost missed it. He stepped back. Dante nudged between them, sitting down on her feet.

She lifted her hand, wanting to tell Yaniv she hadn't meant to hurt him. But after what just happened with Rafael...after all she'd suffered from her stepfather...

How did she overcome all that to trust even this man?

He turned and held out his arm. "Let me escort you to Helida's room. I'm sure the baby is ready for your attention."

Claws clicked on the wood floor. A cool nose nudged her hand. Dante sat beside her and lifted his paw. Maya couldn't stop her smile. She leaned down to take the extended foot and hugged the mutt. His tail swept against the wall.

"Thank you." She buried her face in the dog's fur as she gave him a hug.

"At this moment, I am wishing to turn myself into a dog. That is not something I ever considered before." Amusement tinged Yaniv's voice. She glanced up and noted the crinkles at the corners of his eyes. What kind of man would treat a woman this way? With such compassion?

She stood up and took his proffered arm, knowing the answer. The kind of man she wanted to know better. If only she could relax her guard enough to trust him. Right now, she felt comfortable alone in his presence, but she suspected that had to do with Dante being here.

At the door to Helida's room, he stopped and pulled her to face him. Dante wedged between them, sitting on her feet again, his gaze on Yaniv.

Yaniv's mouth twitched as he looked down. "I'm glad you have such a protector. I will see that Rafael doesn't bother you again." He sighed and shook his head. "Who am I fooling? Helida will see to that."

"Thank you." Her throat tightened as she thought of what might have happened—would have happened—if Yaniv hadn't shown up that day in Los Angeles. How could she ever repay him for saving her life and giving her a future? Leya's wise words came to mind, and she knew all she could do was thank him.

"Maya." He edged a step closer, his boots nudging against Dante's feet. He brushed his fingers along her jaw. She could feel the touch prickling across her scalp and down to her heart.

"Maya, I have never been drawn to a woman before. I…" He paused, his warm gaze holding her until she couldn't breathe. He cleared his throat. "I won't ever force you to do anything you don't want to do. But know this. I want to protect you, to stay close and make sure you are safe. You make me feel things I've never felt before." He leaned forward to brush a light kiss on her forehead, then let her go, and stepped away.

She watched him leave the way they had come. He didn't look back, not even as he turned the corner. She sagged against Helida's door. Her lips tingled as if he'd kissed her. Part of her wished he had. She wanted to be ready for a kiss someday. She did.

Dante leaned against her legs and nudged her knee with his nose. She turned the handle and let them both into the room. Ana still slept. The other children must already be out with the servants. Maya laid out the items she would need to get Ana ready for the day.

When she finished, she sat on the bed. Dante sat beside her, resting his chin on her knee. Stroking the dog's soft ears, Maya considered the turn her life had taken. She closed her eyes, breathed deeply, and said a prayer of thanks as she waited for the baby to wake.

"Rafael, stop." Helida's pleading tone startled Maya upright. Dante growled. Maya's stomach dropped as she heard the heavy thud of footsteps outside the window.

She slipped to the floor between the wall and the bed, coming to rest right under the window. She snapped her fingers, and Dante trotted around to join her. If Rafael saw the dog, he would know where she was.

"Rafael, please." Helida softened her voice and the footsteps halted. "We … I've done you a disservice, mi hermano. Yaniv is right. Mama and I have indulged you too much. You have to let Maya go. She doesn't care for you the way you do her." She paused. Maya held her breath, waiting to hear Rafael's response.

"I want her. We will marry. She will come to love me." Gravel scraped. She pictured him turning to face his sister. "How is this so different from you marrying? You didn't even know *tu esposo* before your wedding day. You've come to love him. She will learn to love me."

Maya could almost see the way his lower lip stuck out in a pout. Rafael might be a man on the outside, but on the inside, he still needed to grow up.

"Mi esposo never forced me to do anything. He has always treated me with kindness and love. Can you say that about the way you've treated Maya? Is trying to buy her from her father treating her with love and kindness?"

Silence. An inaudible growl rumbled through Dante. She felt the vibration as he pressed against her.

"Go away from here, Rafael." Helida's tone went from anger to sorrow. Her hurt brought tears to Maya's eyes. "Go away and see what God has for you. Don't waste your life—and Maya's—this way."

# CHAPTER TEN

YANIV LEANED against the back of the house as he watched Rafael stalk toward the stables. He hadn't meant to eavesdrop. He'd intended to come out here and give his brother a piece of his mind. But Helida did a much better job than his outright confrontation would have done. Though her words were peppered with admonition, her love and mercy shone through.

"God, please let Rafael hear from You. He needs to find You, not try to please Helida or me—or himself." At the crunch of footsteps on the path, Yaniv turned.

Helida approached, wiping her eyes with the tips of her fingers. Her bowed shoulders spoke louder than words.

"Mi hermana." He stepped away from the wall into the path.

Helida gasped and jerked to a stop. Her head snapped up, eyes shining with moisture.

"Did you hear?" She pressed her fingers to her mouth.

"I heard part. I started to say something but thought he would resent me being here." Yaniv took her hands in his. "You said just the right things. Thank you."

"But I hurt him." She hiccupped a little sob.

"I know." He pulled her close and patted her back. "When the wound heals, he will be stronger. Pray God heals his soul. Pray he hears and knows the voice of God."

"You're right. He needs Jesus the most." She sniffed as she stepped back. "I'd better help Maya get the niños ready for their breakfast. Thank you."

She slipped around him and disappeared through the door into the house. Before the door swung shut, he caught the morning noises of children laughing and pans clattering.

He paused. Part of him wanted to seek out Maya, but she would be helping Helida with the children, and that might mean chaos. Instead, he turned toward the barn and the corrals. Maybe he could find Rafael and encourage him. Doubts swirled. He and his brother never managed to be civil to one another. Still...maybe this time.

A light breeze tickled the hair at the nape of his neck. A few clouds chugged across the sky. Lucio stood at the corral chatting with the black stallion—or that's how it looked. Lucio's lips were moving, and no one else stood within hearing distance.

As Yaniv approached, Lucio glanced over his shoulder. He nodded, his expression solemn. "What happened to your hermano? He acted like he had a pack of coyotes on his tail."

"Helida." Yaniv huffed out a chuckle.

"Ah, a sister." Lucio grinned. "Worse than a pack of coyotes."

The stallion nudged Lucio's shoulder before it backed up a step to sniff at Yaniv, who patted the horse's sleek neck. Such a powerful animal. Across the way, Yaniv saw Rosalinda sashaying toward the hacienda. Lucio followed her with his gaze. Yaniv opened his mouth to say something but didn't. What Lucio thought of the flirtatious woman was his business, not Yaniv's. Why he allowed a woman like that on his rancho would be his business too.

A horse snorted. The sound of agitated hoofbeats came from the front of the barn. Lucio frowned as he swiveled to look. Yaniv followed his gaze but couldn't see a thing from this angle.

"I need to see what is happening." Lucio rubbed the black's nose and headed toward the sound of scuffling. Yaniv fell in beside him.

Rafael's gelding danced aside as he lifted the saddle. Yaniv noted the look of frustration on his brother's face. Undoubtedly, the animal sensed anger and reacted to that emotion. Yaniv had never seen Rafael abuse an animal, but he rarely took their sensitivity into consideration.

Before he could berate his hermano, Lucio spoke up. "Let me help." In two strides, Lucio had the lead rope in hand, his palm cupped over the gelding's nose. "Easy."

Yaniv bit down on his tongue to hold back the torrent of words that pushed to get out. This wasn't the time for him to say anything, so he prayed. For Lucio to ask the right questions. For his brother to calm down. For his relationship with Rafael to be healed.

"Where are you going so early?" Lucio's gentle touch held the mount in place.

Rafael lifted the saddle, his shoulders more relaxed, although his eyes still narrowed when he glanced at Yaniv. "I am leaving." His clipped tone made it clear he didn't want to talk.

"Breakfast will be ready in a few minutes." Lucio glanced at the hacienda as the bell rang, almost as if the cook heard his declaration. "You should have a good meal before you leave. And some food to take with you."

"I'll be fine." Rafael yanked the cinch strap tight. The gelding's ears went straight back, and he snorted.

Lucio spoke a few low words, and the horse settled. He glanced at Rafael. "Are you heading home? Yaniv said you all would leave tomorrow."

Rafael dropped the stirrup back down as he finished with the saddle. He snatched up the bridle and slipped it in place, despite the gelding lifting his head high to avoid the bit. "I'll go where I feel like going. It's none of your business. I know you are only asking because Yaniv wants to know."

He swung into the saddle and glared down at Yaniv. "She's yours. I don't care anymore. I'm done with our family." He jerked the horse around, dug in his heels, and galloped from the yard.

"I'm sorry, mi amigo." Lucio rested his hand on Yaniv's shoulder.

Yaniv nodded, unable to speak. A plethora of emotions swirled through him. Relief his brother was gone. Guilt for feeling that way. Fear for what would happen to Rafael. Dread at what to tell Helida and how this would devastate her.

"Let's go to breakfast. We can all pray for him." Lucio led the way to the house.

Inside the laughter and chatter of children lightened Yaniv's mood. He loved his nieces and nephews so much. They always brought a smile, even when they were being ornery. They passed the room where the children were being served and went on to the formal dining room to join the family.

Yaniv tried not to look at his brother's chair as he took his place beside Maya. Her cheeks flushed as he dropped into his chair, but she didn't look at him.

From Maya's other side, Helida mouthed, *Rafael?*

Yaniv glanced down at Maya. She toyed with her food.

He met Helida's gaze, shook his head, and mouthed the answer. *Gone.*

Her eyes widened, and tears glistened, one slipping down her cheek. She brushed it away and turned her attention to her food. Yaniv held back a sigh. He would work hard today to prepare to leave tomorrow.

They needed to get home.

He bowed his head as Lucio led the family in prayer. When Lucio asked God to be with Rafael as he traveled today, Yaniv heard Maya's quiet gasp. While people began to pass the food, Maya gazed up at him with eyes the size of the full moon, a silent question radiating from her.

He nodded. "He left just before the meal. He won't bother you again."

Maya relaxed. Peace shone in her face, and she patted her hand against her thigh.

Something moved near his boot. He started and glanced down to see Dante at her feet, nose lifted to nudge at her fingers. Yaniv's lips twitched. How many people seated at this table knew the stinky beast from last night now hid in this dining room?

"He insisted on being here. After this morning in the garden, he won't leave my side." Maya shot Yaniv a glance from under her lashes. Clearly, she expected his wrath to fall on her and on her dog.

He winked at her. "Then we will have to be quiet and sneak him out when the meal is over."

Her eyes rounded, and she turned her attention back to her plate. Her teeth worried her lower lip for a moment, and then she began to eat.

He tucked eggs and peppers into his tortilla and leaned close to her. "I understand Dante's need to be close to you. I am suffering the same need."

She jumped, so he straightened and took a bite. Her fork clinked against her plate. Conversation drifted around them, and no one seemed to notice their little interchange.

"Maya, I need to talk with you. Will you walk with me after the meal is finished?" He waited until her chin bobbed. He would ask Helida to accompany them to the garden so Maya would feel comfortable. Rafael had meant his parting words to be a taunt. He would never want Yaniv to be with Maya, but Yaniv would no longer deny he loved her. And if he'd been reading her right …

She loved him too.

When most of the family started to leave the dining room, Maya's hand strayed under the table to pet Dante. Yaniv didn't think anyone else in the room could hear the low rumble of warning the dog issued. He felt the sound more than heard it. Maya's caress on the dog's head stopped the rumble.

"Helida." Yaniv beckoned to his hermana. She leaned closer to hear him.

"Would you accompany us on a walk in the garden?" His face warmed under the knowing gleam in his sister's eye. "Maybe the servants would watch your niños for a few more minutes."

Her lips twitched. Beside him, Maya's cheeks flushed, and her hand stilled on Dante's head. Yaniv tried not to be jealous of a mutt—to little success. Would she return his love? If so, maybe one day soon he would be the recipient of her tender touch.

As they rounded the end of the table, Helida burst out laughing. "I can't believe you brought that dog in here. At least he smells better today." She hugged Maya and held out her fingers toward Dante. The dog sniffed her, his tail thumping against Yaniv's leg. Amazing how fast Dante had adjusted to people once Maya earned his trust.

"Maya and I should grab our shawls." Helida gestured toward their rooms. "The wind this morning is brisk."

Maya followed her down the hall. Yaniv watched them, leaning against the wall, his eyes never leaving the long braid swaying against Maya's back. Dante padded after her.

After Maya ducked into her room, Helida continued walking. He waited, watching for Maya. His heart did a slow roll as he thought of what he wanted to ask her. Was it too soon? Would he upset her? He did not want to pressure her. He wanted this to be her choice. But he prayed she would choose him.

Helida emerged, wrapping her rebozo around her shoulders. The satiny material, embroidered with flowers and vines, was a work of art. He thought of Maya's simple rebozo, a plain white shawl made of coarse cloth. He wanted to get her something beautiful. As beautiful as Helida's.

His sister paused outside Maya's door. Her head tilted to one side. She put her hand over her mouth, her eyes wide when she turned to look at Yaniv.

Something was amiss.

He strode toward her, his pulse thrumming.

Maya had left the door cracked open. He could hear voices within. Not Maya talking to Dante, but the low tones of a man's voice.

A voice he knew all too well.

Anger washed over him. He started to push the door open, but Helida caught his arm. Her eyes pleaded with him. For what? Compassion on a brother who deserved to be thrashed?

*Pray.*

His wise hermana mouthed the word. Shame washed over him. He closed his eyes for a moment to ask for help and eased the door wide enough to see into the room.

Rafael held onto Maya's arm, tugging her toward the window.

She pulled back. "Let me go! I am not leaving with you." She pried at his fingers, but he didn't release her. "Yaniv and Lucio said you left."

"I tricked them." Rafael yanked her to him. "I would not leave without my most precious possession." His expression darkened. "You will come to care for me. We are leaving now and will be married by nightfall. You will be mine."

"I will *never* be yours. Any man who hurts an animal doesn't deserve to be loved." Maya sent a glance over her shoulder. For the first time, Yaniv noted Dante lying on the floor. What had his brother done?

Beside him, Helida moaned.

"It was only a little kick to the head. He'll be fine." Rafael swiveled toward the doorway, and his gaze collided with Yaniv's. His mouth turned up in a sneer. "I see we didn't get away fast enough. It doesn't matter, hermano. You can't stop me."

Helida stepped in front of Yaniv. "Rafael. Don't do this."

Enough. Yaniv strode toward his brother and Maya as Helida slipped from the room. He knew she would call for Lucio to bring men to help.

"Let her go, Rafael. She doesn't want to marry you."

"She will change her mind." The muscles in Rafael's jaw flexed.

Yaniv kept his gaze on his brother's face. He saw the sudden hesitation in Rafael's eyes. The little boy who always wanted more, who wanted approval above anything else.

And the disbelief a second before Yaniv's fist crashed into his jaw.

Yaniv caught Maya as Rafael fell to the floor. He pulled her to him, and she buried her head against his chest. Rafael didn't get up, but he wouldn't be out for long.

"Let's check Dante." Yaniv turned Maya toward her dog.

Dante sat up, shook his head, and licked Maya's hand as she sank down to pet him.

"Let's go." Yaniv helped her up. Dante surged to his feet. Wobbled a little. Licked Maya's hand again. As Lucio and Ramón hurried in, Yaniv led Maya from the room. Behind them, Rafael groaned.

# CHAPTER ELEVEN

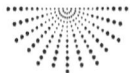

MAYA STOOD beside Helida at the edge of the garden, watching Lucio and Ramón hustle Rafael to the stable. Yaniv strode alongside Lucio, his back straight, shoulders rigid. One of Lucio's men followed with Rafael's horse. The men stopped outside the barn doors.

She could watch no longer. She had to make her trembling legs work and get away. To her room? With the horrible memories? The garden bench? She shivered.

Not there either.

Dante nudged her thigh with his nose. He had one paw on her foot as he leaned against her. What comfort he offered. And protection! He'd bought her enough time earlier that Yaniv and Helida found her before Rafael dragged her away. Truly, Dante was a gift from God.

She touched Helida's arm and murmured that she was going back in the house. In her room, she shuddered at the signs of the struggle that had taken place. Dante whined and licked her hand.

*I am not afraid.*

The words rang through her. How she wanted to embrace them.

She crossed to the far wall where an armoire rested. Opening the door of the large wardrobe, she climbed inside and huddled beneath the hanging clothes. She'd found safety during her childhood in such a place. Dante stayed outside, her ever-present sentinel.

She pressed clothing to her face to muffle the sound of her sobs. Sobs of terror and questioning why this happened to…

But as she wept, something changed. Her mourning became praise and thanksgiving. God had been there. He hadn't let her down. Leya had spoken true. God *would* watch over her. He had done so. More bad things might happen, but God would be with her to see her through.

As this truth washed over her, Maya rested her forehead on her drawn-up knees and basked in His presence.

AN HOUR LATER, Maya washed her face, hoping to erase some ravages of tears, and left her room with Dante trailing at her heels. The house was quieter than usual. She may have missed their mid-day meal but wasn't hungry. As she stepped outside, Yaniv surged up from a bench beside the door. He yanked off his hat, his fingers kneading the brim.

"Are you all right? I wanted Helida to check on you, but she said to give you time. I…" He stopped, licked his lips, and seemed at a loss for what to say.

"Is he truly gone this time?" Maya hesitated to ask Yaniv about his brother, but she had to know. She'd thought Rafael was gone before, but it hadn't been true.

Sorrow etched fine lines around Yaniv's eyes. "You are not at fault for all that has happened between Rafael and me."

But if not for her, maybe he and his brother would not be in this situation. Maybe Helida wouldn't be red-eyed from weeping, as she'd been when Maya left to go inside.

Yaniv's tone was firm. "He's gone. Ramón will ride with him to the next rancho. I don't know where Rafael will go from there, but he knows he is not welcome to return. Not here. And not to our home."

Yaniv took her hands in his. His touch spread warmth through her chilled body, easing some of the tension that returned when she'd stepped outside.

"Will you walk with me in the garden? I believe Helida will join us." He lifted Maya's hands and brushed a light kiss along the back of her knuckles.

Awareness shivered through her. She nodded, unable to speak.

The sun shone brightly as they ambled down the path. A bee buzzed past her to land on a nearby flower. The children's laughter floated on the breeze and lifted some of the pall that had settled over her since this morning. Dante whined beside her. She heard the whinny of the mare, so she patted the dog, releasing him, then smiled as the beast raced off toward the barn.

Yaniv put his hand on top of hers where it lay tucked in the crook of his elbow. His smile held such promise. He walked down the closest path, but she tugged on his arm until he stopped. He half-turned to face her, his eyebrows raised.

"Please." She cleared her throat and tried again. "Please, will you forgive me?" She held her breath, watching the play of emotions run across his handsome features.

"Why should I forgive you when you have done nothing wrong? I can't think of any way you have offended or hurt me." He stepped closer and cupped her cheek. "What do you think you have done?"

"Rafael." She wanted just for a moment to lean into his touch. "Because of Rafael." Tears burned behind her eyes. She did not want to cry. Must not cry.

He shook his head and closed his eyes. Leaned forward until his forehead touched hers. One hand lifted to smooth a strand of hair behind her ear. "Did you entice my brother at all? Did you promise him you would care for him or ask him to take you away?"

She started back a step, and his hand dropped. "No. *Never.*"

"Then why would you be at fault?" His lips tilted in a small smile. "I imagine you did your best to avoid Rafael when he visited your house."

She nodded.

"Then you are not at fault for anything. I am sad my brother caused this rift. Maybe I could have done something to change him, but I don't know what. Our conflict has been building for years." He tugged her closer. "I can only pray that he finds his way to God. If you want to help, you can join Helida and me in praying for him."

"Every day. I will pray for him every day." Would it be bad, though, to pray that Rafael would find God in some other part of the country than where she might be?

Yaniv walked, and she fell into step beside him. The children's squeals grew as they neared the center of the garden and the stone bench where she liked to sit.

Helida waved to them. She and Leya sat on the bench, and she held Ana in her lap as they watched the children play. Claudio sat in the dirt stacking pieces of wood on one another until they fell. When they did, he laughed so hard everyone joined in.

Darío and his sister, Marciana, were taking turns walking on their hands while the other held up the legs. Maya snorted a laugh as five-year-old Marciana struggled to hold her brother's legs, and they both tipped on their sides.

Maya swallowed hard. Oh, to have memories of playing with her brothers like this. Foolery, Bruno had always said, was not for them. Nothing good came from playing when there was work to be done. But now…watching these children…

Maya realized that hadn't been true at all.

Yaniv stopped before they entered the clearing and leaned close to speak to her. "I see how you light up when you look at the niños. Someday you will have little ones, yes?"

She stared up at him, lost for a moment in the warmth of his eyes. Her heart did a slow roll, and for the first time, she let herself admit the truth. She loved this man! She could trust him when she could trust no one else. He cared about his family and protected them without being demanding and harsh. Even with Rafael, he showed restraint compared to the men she'd known growing up.

"Have you seen the pond?" Yaniv gestured to a branch of the path Maya hadn't noticed before.

She shook her head.

"Let's go see." He turned them and waved at Helida and Leya. "We'll be back in a few minutes."

"I want to go, Tío." Marciana jumped up and raced toward them. Darío shrugged and moved over to help Claudio stack wood pieces.

"Come on. You can lead the way." Yaniv let his niece race past them. "Don't get too far ahead. And don't jump in the water." He grinned down at Maya. "That girl is part fish. If there is water around, she is wet."

"I like that," Maya said. "I used to sneak away to the river near us. I had to be careful not to get too wet or Bruno would—" Heat surged into her face at what she'd been about to say.

"Maya." Yaniv slowed their pace.

Marciana trotted back around a corner to check on them and crossed her arms over her chest.

Yaniv ignored the little girl's clear demand that they hurry along. "Maya, I have so much I want to say to you. I know you had a difficult life with Bruno and his sons. I'm sorry my brother was a part of that."

Marciana stamped her foot.

Yaniv fought a smile, shook his head, and continued down the path.

Maya's skin tingled. What did he want to say to her? Had he realized she would be a hindrance at his rancho? Dread prickled along her spine. If he wanted to be rid of her, she would beg Lucio to allow her to stay and work here. She couldn't go back.

Dante raced up behind her, sniffed the air, nudged her hand, and trotted ahead. They rounded a curve and saw Marciana crouched beside a small pool. Plants grew in profusion along the edge. Water trickled over a few rocks, the sound almost musical.

Maya gasped. She'd never seen anything so beautiful, a spot so peaceful.

A bench similar to the one she'd shared with Leya sat at the end of the oblong pool. Yaniv led her there and they sat.

"May I put my feet in the water?" Marciana's eyes were big and pleading.

Maya covered her mouth to keep from letting the girl see her smile.

"Only if you take your shoes off first." Yaniv spoke in a stern tone, but she noted the humor in his eyes.

Maya laughed as Marciana hurried to remove her shoes and stockings.

"This is so beautiful." She leaned down to dip her fingers in the cool water. She wished she could take her shoes off and dip her feet in too. Dante trotted over, his tongue still dripping, and flopped down at her feet.

"Maya." Yaniv turned to face her on the bench. He clasped her hands in his, pulling her closer to him. Her heart pounded. Being this close to him made her long for things she shouldn't. Long for his arms around her. Long for a kiss. For his love.

"I don't want you to think I am like Rafael."

Her mouth fell open. "You are not at *all* like him."

Relief flitted across his face. His shoulders lost their stiffness. "Thank you. Because what I have to say could not be said if you compared me to him."

"What?" She leaned a little closer, drawn by something she couldn't deny.

"I love you." Eagerness lit his eyes.

She couldn't look away. He *loved* her?

A surge of warmth sent her pulse racing. She didn't know what to say. He loved her. Yaniv Madrigal loved her! How could that be? She wanted to jump up and down. To run back to Helida and Leya and say, "Yaniv *loves* me!"

"I know you may not be ready. I don't want to rush you. I will never force you to do anything you don't want to, so if you don't feel the same way about me, I will understand."

He was...*nervous.* She felt the tremors in his hands as he kept talking nonsense about her not wanting him.

Maya pulled her hands free. Yaniv looked down, drew back. But before he could move too far, she reached up to frame his face in her palms. She might not know what life had in store for her, but she knew this.

She loved Yaniv. Wanted more than anything to spend the rest of her life with him.

She tugged his head down and raised herself up to give him a soft kiss. He moaned. Put his arms around her and pulled her close. He tilted his head and kissed her back, not the sweet brush of lips as she'd done, but a real kiss. A kiss that proclaimed, "I love you."

"Mama. Yaniv is kissing Maya. Ewwww." Marciana's shrill cry broke them apart.

Yaniv grinned. Maya pressed her face to his chest.

"Ah, I love you, Maya." He whispered the words for her hearing only.

She leaned back to look up at him. "I love you too, Yaniv."

Dante shoved his head between them and put his front paws on Maya's lap. She and Yaniv both laughed.

"Will you marry me, Maya?"

Yaniv's soft question halted her laughter. He wanted her as his wife. Her, an esclava. A slave. A woman who'd been set free from so many horrors and given a gift of love. Yaniv's love. His sister's love. Most of all, God's love, something she learned to appreciate more each day.

"Yes." She blinked away moisture at the joy on his face. "Yes, I will marry you, Yaniv."

He leaped to his feet, picked her up, and twirled her around.

"Tío, what are you doing?" Marciana splashed her feet in the pond and droplets splattered around them.

"I just asked Maya to marry me. You are going to have a new Tía." He grinned as his *sobrina* scrambled to her feet. Leaving her shoes and stockings, she raced down the path yelling their news.

Yaniv grinned. "I'd say let's go tell my sister, but that seems to have been done for us." He gave Maya a quick kiss, snatched up his niece's shoes and stockings, and escorted his *novia* down the path to where his friends and family waited. In the midst of hugs and welcome-to-the-family wishes, Maya marveled.

Her dream of having a real family had come true.

*Thank you, Jesus.*

She squeezed Yaniv's hand, and he smiled down at her as if he knew her thoughts. For the first time, she welcomed that idea. The idea of them becoming one in marriage meant becoming one in thoughts too. What a wonderful gift.

# GLOSSARY

Abuelo(a) – Grandfather/mother

Amigo(s) – Friend(s)

Amor – Love

Ándele – Come on, Hurry up

Bandolero – Bandit

(La) Bebé – (The) Baby

Caballo(s) – Horse(s)

Caballito - Small horse

Chico – Boy

Compadre(s) – Good friend(s)

Esclava - Slave

Está bien – All right

Familia – Family

Hacienda – House

Hermano(a) – Brother/Sister

(Un) Hombre – (A) man

Madre – Mother

Mañada de Caballos – Herd of Horses

Mantilla/Reboza – Shawl or scarf

Monstuo(s) – Monster(s)

Niño(a) – child

Novia - girlfriend/fiancé

¿Qué pasa? - What is wrong?

Rebozo - Shawl

Señor(a) – Mr./Mrs.

Señores – Sirs

Sobrina - niece

Tía(o) – Aunt/Uncle

Tapar un hoyo y destapar otro - To fill one hold while digging another.

Vaquero – Cowboy

!Ya Basta! – Stop it!

# AUTHOR'S NOTE

People often ask where an author gets the idea for a book. The idea for The Ranchero's Gift was born one Sunday morning when I visited a church. The Pastor told the story of Abraham Lincoln purchasing a slave woman and then setting her free. Instead of leaving and going her way, the woman wanted to go with Abraham Lincoln because he had given her the gift of freedom.

The Pastor then explored the idea of Jesus Christ purchasing us with His blood and then giving us our freedom. I couldn't quit thinking about that freedom and how we react to being set free. I remember wanting to repay God as a new Christian so I incorporated some of that lesson into The Ranchero's Gift.

I am so thankful for Jesus and the gift of freedom He has given me. I hope this story will be the springboard for you, the reader, to consider what Jesus has done for you. How will you respond to this incredible gift?

Nancy J. Farrier

# ACKNOWLEDGMENTS

Writing a book can be a lonely process, but publishing one takes a team. I am so thankful for my team. They come beside me to encourage and guide, to make this story much better than I can do alone.

To my editors, Karen Ball and Louise M. Gouge. Thank you for your changes that shaped my words and thoughts. Louise, thank you for the title suggestion. You are both amazing.

To my team of early readers, Anne Anderson, Alyssa Farrier, Marie Harris and Junie Hostetler. Thank you for catching all the little typos and mistakes and for your encouragement. Junie, thank you for your help with the Spanish.

To my cover designer, Ardra Tsuei. Thank you for the hard work you put in, for reading the story and expressing my ideas in a cover that isas the first thing people see.

To my husband, Robert John Farrier. Thank you for putting up with such a weird wife. One who talks to people who aren't there, or who zones out in the middle of a conversation when inspiration strikes.

Most of all, thank you to my Lord and Savior, Jesus. Without Him I am nothing. In Him I am all I need to be.

# ABOUT THE AUTHOR

Nancy J. Farrier is a multi-published, award winning author of historical and contemporary Christian fiction. She writes Southwest fiction with real life issues. She lives in Southern Arizona in the Sonoran Desert with her husband, cats and dog. She has five children and six grandchildren. Nancy loves reading, hiking, bicycling, needlework, and spending time with her family.

## ALSO BY NANCY J. FARRIER

Land of Promise Series

The Ranchero's Love

Bandolero

Brides of Arizona

The Cowboy's Bride

A Bride's Agreement

The Timeless Love Romance Collection

8 Weddings and a Miracle

The Immigrant Brides

Painted Desert

www.ingramcontent.com/pod-product-compliance
Lightning Source LLC
Chambersburg PA
CBHW030547130626
46552CB00006B/2460